The Hidden River

Other books of
The Mogi Franklin Mysteries
Ghosts of the San Juan
The Lost Children
The Secret of La Rosa
The Lake of Fire

The Hidden River

Donald Willerton

Terra Nova Books
SANTA FE, NEW MEXICO

Library of Congress Control Number 2017946014

Distributed by SCB Distributors, (800) 729-6423

Terra Nova Books

Published by Terra Nova Books, Santa Fe, New Mexico.
www.TerraNovaBooks.com

ISBN 978-1-938288-80-7

For My Mother

CHAPTER

Acoma Pueblo
Late October, 1692

The man snugged a coarse wool blanket around himself and shivered in the cool breeze of the night, but it was more from fear than cold. Were he to be discovered, he would be whipped for disobedience.

Lying on the roof and placing his ear over the ventilation hole of the *kiva*, the windowless room built for religious and political meetings, he listened to the voices inside. The pueblo leaders had spent several evenings in conversation, but tonight's talk had an urgency that made the voices sound anxious and animated.

A decision could no longer be delayed; action was needed.

The Spanish army had returned to Santa Fe, surrounded those in the village center, and negotiated their surrender. The commander then led his troops to Pecos Pueblo in the east and they had surrendered as well. One by one, other pueblos were visited and, though sometimes needing forceful persuasion, each had given in to the commander's demands. The army was now marching toward the settlements in the west and would soon arrive at Acoma, the pueblo of the Acoma people—the pueblo of the men gathered within the room below the listening man.

When the soldiers came to them and asked for their surrender and obedience to the Spanish king and his religion, what would their answer be?

The Spanish had come to the country of Nuevo Mexico ninety years earlier, savagely conquering the native people, requiring that they obey the Spanish government, and forcing into slavery those who resisted. Once resistance was put down, the people in the various pueblos along the Rio Grande and other regions were punished for their beliefs and practices, pronounced converted to Christianity, and forced to serve the Catholic priests and missionaries.

After suffering years of tyranny and abuse, the pueblos had banded together and rebelled against the Spanish rule. More than four hundred soldiers, missionaries, priests, men, women, and children were killed. Fields and homes were burned, mission churches were profaned and destroyed, and the government in Santa Fe was overthrown. Any escaping Spaniards fled south to Mexico.

After the revolt, the pueblos should have strengthened the bond created by their common suffering, but they did not. They returned to squabbling and competing, and to tribal politics. They grew disgusted with one another, began new battles among the tribes, and returned to their isolated practices.

Now, twelve years after the rebellion, the Spanish were returning to retake what they considered to be their land and, again, to place the pueblos under their rule. The pueblo leaders knew that no matter how much the Spanish leader might talk about peace and coexistence, the soldiers and settlers would neither forget nor forgive what had happened during the revolt. The Spanish would again become tyrants.

Pulling the blanket tighter over his head, the man outside the kiva focused on the words of the governor, the highest official of the Acoma community.

"We have the blood holder," he said. "When the blood holder was in the hands of the Spaniards, we suffered shame and hunger and death. When the blood holder was in our hands, we became one people and obeyed only ourselves."

Alternating between argument and lecture, the governor emphasized the magical power of the blood holder and how that power had helped them. "The blood holder brings us favor in the eyes of the Spanish god. We must not let it go. We must treasure it and protect it and keep it from the Spaniards. It must be taken to a place where they cannot find it."

The man outside grew angry. Such useless talk! Power was meant to be used, not hidden!

Thinking of what might happen with the return of the Spaniards had brought panic and dread. The Spaniards were vicious and cruel and enjoyed the miseries they caused. With their return, the suffering would begin again.

The only hope was that the blood holder would protect them. But no one knew how the magic worked. Must the blood holder be held in the middle of battle or did the magic work from far away? Would it cause the enemy to fall? Would their blood weaken and craziness come upon them? Would the Acoma people grow great strength and turn away the flying metal that spit from the weapons of the soldiers?

What if it were captured by the Spaniards? Would the pain and suffering of the Acoma be greater?

Back and forth, moving from passionate belief to strict reasoning, from hope to fear, the talking went on until the moon passed high overhead. Struggling, still divided on what to do, the urgency for action finally forced a decision: With the coming of the day, the governor would take the blood holder to the Womb of the Mother, the location of their most sacred rituals. It would be safe there. Only he, and the old ones, knew the secret path through the black rocks. Once hidden, the Spaniards would never know that the blood holder even existed.

Fools, the man listening at the vent hole thought. They are all fools! He rose and slipped into the shadows.

The governor stood proud in the sunrise of the next day. He was now the Honored One, the Guardian, the Deliverer. A wooden box held the blood holder cradled in soft deerskin. Wrapped in a blanket, the box was placed into a sling with food, water, and other essentials he would need on his journey.

Going past worried faces, he moved through the winding lanes among the apartment-style adobe houses and picked his way down the steep steps to the valley below. Grave eyes watched from the mesa's rim as the governor moved across the fields and disappeared into the canyons in the west.

The pueblo, constructed of mud and rock brought from the valley floor, had always been considered safe from its enemies. A few hundred families lived on the flat rock top of a mesa that rose four hundred feet straight up out of the valley. A stranger attempting to enter the village was met with sheer cliffs of solid sandstone. There was only one way to the top, and it was hidden: a series of ladder-like footholds cut into the walls of a crevice between the cliffs, a path where only one person at a time could ascend or descend the mesa's heights.

The villagers watched as their governor passed from their sight, but what they failed to see was that a man had emerged from the shadows of the boulders and rocks of the canyon—the young man who was secretly listening at the kiva the night before—and that he now trailed the governor.

The governor reached the land of hard-walking by late afternoon. He was of one mind, singing under his breath, remembering his prayers and chants. The Womb of the Mother was the most holy place of the Acoma people and was not often visited. Times were bad, indeed, if it now must serve as a hiding place.

But the worry in his mind had vanished with the clean air and the stretching of his legs. The path was clear and the mission understood. He was ready for the next part of his journey, and the air, new and fresh, filled his lungs with expectation. He felt strong.

Moving along the edge of the black rocks until he recognized the faint markings of the trail, he stopped. He removed his moccasins, wrapped his feet in additional layers of deerskin, and laced large yucca sandals around his bundled feet. Then he climbed up and over a ledge and moved into the vastness of the harsh land.

The man following him cursed his luck. He had not expected the journey to take him into the land of hard-walking and had only the leather moccasins he wore daily. Moving onto the unusual rocks to follow his unsuspecting guide, he felt the sharp edges beneath his toes.

It was twilight before the governor found what he was looking for. With a sigh of relief, he placed his sling on the ground and then spread out his blankets. He would spend the night outside the Womb of the Mother and place his precious package on the altar tomorrow.

Even though there was little soil, many grasses, bushes, and trees grew from the sand and dirt brought by the wind. He selected a dry brush with a thick stem and long roots, pulled the plant from the ground, peeled the roots back onto the stem, and used pieces of rawhide to wrap them into a thick rod. With the roots to creating a tight crown on one end, it would serve as a torch to light the dark spaces of the Womb. He finished three more torches and laid them close to his side. He then slid between his blankets and was soon asleep.

The other man was in pain. The thin hide of his moccasins had ripped within the first mile. He attempted to protect his feet by cutting the fibrous leaves of yucca plants and hastily weaving them into coverings that he tied around his leg with rawhide strips. But, poorly done, the edges caught and frayed, the rawhide pulled from its ties, and the weaving fell apart. He had no choice but to continue on and bear the pain as his feet were cut and bruised.

Thankfully, he was still within sight of the old man as he stopped and prepared his camp for the night. Memorizing the appearance of the hill and the surrounding land, the spy knew he could find it again. Relieved that the chase was over, the exhausted man crept to a better view and then hid himself behind a clump of rabbit brush, settling into a guarded vigil.

Hours later, the darkness of night gave way to dawn. The spy had not wanted to sleep, afraid that the governor might make an unexpected move, but the sun was high when the man snapped awake. Hurrying to look over the bushes, he saw that the older man was gone.

Panicking, the spy anxiously searched the older man's campsite—the blankets, sling, and footwear all remained, so his adversary had not left and had to be close by. There were faint tracks in a stretch of hard sand, but it was the smell that made him pause and raise his head—the faint aroma of smoke. Slowly scanning his surroundings, he glimpsed a wisp of darkness against the sky and followed it toward a patch of large yucca growing against a line of rocks.

Seeing some of the leaves pushed aside, he discovered that they hid an opening between the rocks and the sand—an opening into a small cave. Kneeling and warily crawling in, he understood the necessity of the torches that the governor had prepared. It was not a cave but an entrance to a passageway that grew larger and darker as it twisted around the rocks. The man could crawl only a few steps before the light behind him grew too dim to go on.

If he made torches, he could go farther, but if he were discovered, the governor would retrieve the blood holder and return it to the village. That would ruin everything.

He turned around.

Before he was fully out of the entrance, he detected another scent coming from the darkness of the passageway. It was a powerful smell, and it excited his mind. He took a deep breath. The ancient tales were true!

Backing out through the yucca plants, wiping away his own tracks as best he could, the spy picked his way onto the surrounding rock and returned to where he had left his pack. Knowing he would not be spending another night, he cut his blanket into strips and wrapped his feet. He would return to the village, bandage his feet properly, make better preparations, and then return to retrieve the magic object that would permit him to lead his people to victory.

He limped off toward the pueblo.

*   *   *

The governor, having entered the sacred place, put the object into the altar and then returned to gather his things to start back. Hours later, he camped that evening in the canyons. He wanted to arrive when the sun of the new day would greet him as he completed his quest.

The next morning, as the governor climbed the steps to the top of the mesa, the people welcomed him with shouts and drums. Following him as he passed by, the villagers moved to the east end of the isolated mesa to celebrate.

They did not see the Spanish soldiers who had camped to the north of the valley floor and had secretly made their way across the fields. As the governor was being hailed in the streets above, soldiers were making their way to the crevice below. The army had come to the Acoma region sooner than expected, and its scouts had watched the governor as he climbed the secret pathway.

Leaving their heavy metal breastplates and other protection stacked at the bottom of the path, the soldiers climbed the steps quietly, their swords and guns cinched on their backs. They numbered less than a hundred, facing a village of more than a thousand. Their intent was not to do battle but to firmly and resolutely offer the terms of Diego de Vargas, their commander and the new Spanish governor of the region.

The first ones up secreted themselves and waited for all the soldiers to ascend the stairway. When together, marshaling their arms, forming into ranks and boldly marching down the streets, the soldiers sang a cadence to their pace. The rhythmic sound was soon heard at the far end of the mesa, and the celebration chants, prayers, and songs of the Acoma people fell into a deathly silence.

Only one man of the pueblo had seen the soldiers and watched as they climbed the steps. It was the spy, the man who had followed the elder to the secret place, and who had returned for supplies. He lay hidden until the soldiers marched by, then grabbed his pack, slipped through an upper door, dropped into the street from a wall, and made quickly down the pathway for the fields below.

This time, he remembered the foot wrappings and yucca sandals.

Once past the fields and into the canyons, he slowed to a hobble, his feet not yet healed. He pushed ahead, desperate to seek the Womb of the Mother, to find the weapon, and to return to save the village.

His escape, however, did not go unnoticed.

The troops spread out as the negotiations began, and a solitary soldier noticed the man scurrying west across the flatlands below the mesa. The man, no doubt, was racing to spread the news of the soldiers' arrival to the other villages to the west. Reporting the escape to his captain, the sergeant was assigned to retrieve the man after the negotiations were finished. Acquainted with the hard land in front of the escaping man, the captain knew it would take him many hours to travel out of their reach. Waiting until morning to begin a chase would be soon enough.

It satisfied the sergeant. An experienced soldier, seasoned in the campaigns of the new world, he knew how to track and he knew how to be patient when chasing slaves. The man was on foot, whereas the soldier would have his horse. And the man even looked to be injured. There was no hurry.

Confident in his skills and his horse's strength, the soldier never imagined the power he was about to encounter.

CHAPTER

Present Day

"**A**re you crazy?" a man shouted.

Mogi Franklin jerked up from a slouch in his auditorium seat.

"You're an idiot! I'm not listening to this garbage!" another man spat at the speaker.

"You have insulted my people!" yelled another.

Half the audience was on its feet. Some people shouted, pointing angrily and shaking their fists while others talked heatedly to those around them.

Mogi yanked out his ear buds and turned to his sister, Jennifer. They were sitting with their mom and dad, having come in from the campground to attend the evening talk hosted by the National Park Service. They were traveling in their RV for a few days of vacation and had camped at El Malpais National Monument south of Grants, New Mexico.

"What? What did he say?"

"He called them cannibals," she responded. "The ancestors of the Acoma Pueblo, specifically, but basically all the Pueblo Indians. Said they ate the flesh of their enemies and drank their blood."

In the midst of the audience's violent reaction, the speaker seemed shocked and insulted. "I understand it might be hard to accept," he continued, growing more agitated as he spoke. "But my research is good and I've done it well. If you can't be civil, please leave."

Several people got up and stormed out, slamming their seats and continuing to shout both at the speaker and the monument superintendent. A stream of people walked past the front of the auditorium, calling the speaker blind, stupid, crazy, and many other harsh names. The speaker yelled back at them until the superintendent moved him away from the microphone and calmed him down.

In a few minutes, the remaining audience quieted enough for the speaker—Professor Richard Chandler from the University of Eastern Iowa—to continue. He returned to the microphone. "The truth can be hard sometimes," he said, his voice rising. "But my goal this summer is to find absolute proof that the ancestors of the present-day Pueblo Indians were both murderers and cannibals."

Chandler—tall, thin, and gaunt-looking—was the perfect image of a nerd scientist: rumpled clothes, pants too short, a thin tie off center around an unbuttoned collar, and a shock of unkempt hair offset by eyes half-hidden by thick lenses.

After provoking his audience with his introduction, the professor settled down and continued with his talk, showing photographs to explain the basis of his research. He projected an image of an old Spanish document written in very dense handwriting.

"Examining documents in Mexico City, I found a story written in 1732 that tells of a conversation between a father and his son, both slaves serving the household of Antonio Flores de Salaz, a wealthy Mexican trader who lived north of

Mexico City. The father had been born and raised at Acoma Pueblo before he was captured and taken to Mexico."

This brought a buzz from the audience, several of whom were from Acoma Pueblo, the historical home of the Acoma people, not more than twenty miles away. Spread across a half-million acres with a population of about five thousand living in three separate villages, the original, ancient village of the Pueblo was called Sky City because it had been built high on top of an isolated mesa.

"The writing is hard to read and even harder to translate. I will paraphrase what the father told the son," Chandler said.

"When the Spanish army returned to Santa Fe in 1692 to resettle the area, many of the pueblos believed they would be punished for having participated in the revolt, and several of them prepared for war. But the Acoma Pueblo had a secret object that they believed would protect them. The object had magical powers.

"Not knowing how to use the magic, the Pueblo leaders hid the object in a holy place known only to the elders. But before they could discover its use, the Spanish army came to Acoma, negotiated a peace, and the people were returned to Spanish rule. Still thinking the object might be powerful, they never retrieved it from its hiding place. After a few years, those elders died, and its hiding place was forgotten.

"The conversation between the father and his son continued with the father confessing that he himself had discovered the location of the hiding place and, on the very day that the Spanish soldiers came, set out to retrieve it. He thought he knew how to use its magic. But he never removed the magical object from its hiding place. Instead he was captured by Spanish troops, taken to Mexico City, and given as a servant to the Salaz household.

"After living for decades as a slave, the father told the story to his son, worried that he would die without passing on the knowledge. The father wrote a riddle describing the location, using descriptors that he explained only to his son.

"But the conversation had been overheard and written down by members of the household. Both the slave and the son were executed for keeping secrets from the master of the house. Neither of them revealed the meaning of the riddle."

The professor displayed an enlargement of another Spanish document. Mogi could make out letters and words even though they were written in very thin script.

"I do not know what the object was or where it was hidden," the professor continued, pausing to drink from a bottle of water. "However, I believe that the object was a ceremonial bowl used in gathering the blood of an enemy, the drinking of which was believed to give great powers to the person who drank it."

It was laughter now that rippled across the audience. It wasn't hard for Mogi to understand why. Not only had Chandler made preposterous statements about a people who lived three hundred years earlier, but he had based his conclusions on an old riddle about something he wouldn't recognize even if it were in front of him.

He had to be nuts!

"You can laugh all you want," the professor went on with undisguised arrogance, "but you will eventually have to recognize and accept what your ancestors were capable of."

I don't like this guy, Mogi thought, but the mystery's kind of cool. An ancient bowl with magical powers!

Chandler brought up another image and said, "This shows the English translation of the riddle."

Mogi leaned forward to read it.

*It was in the land of hard-walking.
Into the Womb of the Mother was the blood holder
placed, beneath the hill in the middle of the land of hard-
walking. In my dreams do I see the opening of the Womb
and smell the thick smell of the river.*

Mogi whipped out his phone and took a photo before the
professor switched to a new image.

"Since the father, in terms of a normal Puebloan's life, had
probably never been far from Acoma, the hiding place must
be somewhere close to the mesa. It is my intention to find the
'Womb of the Mother' and solve the mystery. You, all of you,
are going to have to face up to the fact that your ancestors
were flesh-eating savages!"

The crowd reacted as if he had reached out and slapped
every one of them. Observing the uproar, Dr. Chandler
cracked a haughty smile, gathered his papers, and sat down.
The audience was already out of their seats and moving toward
the door.

There was no applause.

"I hope this guy has a lock on his door tonight," Jennifer
said, watching the faces of people moving toward the exits.
"Might be a good night for a lynching."

Whack!

A sharp sound came from a few rows in front of them.
Mogi's eyes darted toward the seats. A young woman had
leaned over the back of her seat and given a young man a fu-
rious slap across the face. The guy looked like a teenager but
could have been older, the dark features of his Hispanic face
making it hard to guess his age. His hair was slicked back and
he wore a handkerchief folded and wrapped into a headband.
He was holding his cheek with a wide grin.

In contrast, the girl was certainly not Hispanic, with a full head of blond hair pulled back from a light-skinned "Anglo" face. She, too, wore a grin, but her eyes shone with a daring look. The guy, still grinning and holding his face, slinked away toward the exit.

Mogi knew the guy was making light of the hit, but it had to hurt. The girl had delivered one colossal slap.

*   *   *

"It's a bad situation, for sure," the superintendent said.

Bob Toffler had been superintendent of El Malpais National Monument for about five years. Spanish for "the badlands," El Malpais was the name given to hundreds of acres of lava flows in west-central New Mexico that abutted the southern edge of Grants, a small city an hour or so west of Albuquerque.

After the talk, Mogi's dad had approached the superintendent, Mr. Toffler, and introduced the Franklin family. As they shook hands, Mogi noticed a young woman approaching them. It was the same girl who had slapped the boy.

"Hey, welcome to the peaceful city of Grants, everybody," she said. "Let's see if we can get an old-fashioned civil war going!" The woman smiled broadly as she joined the group.

"And this," Mr. Toffler said, "is my daughter, Rachel. I doubt you could visit anywhere in the county and not meet the Shining Star of Grants."

The girl laughed, flashing gleaming white teeth. Mogi didn't mean to stare, but felt his face growing warm. She was downright beautiful. Older than Jennifer by one or two years, she was probably eighteen or nineteen.

"She's obviously capable of holding her own with the local boy population," Mr. Toffler added, glancing at his daughter.

The girl laughed. "I'm not sure about the shining star part, but I can hold my own," Rachel said as she greeted the Franklin family. "And I do manage to make sure the bulls stay in their pastures and behave themselves."

She was especially happy to meet Jennifer. "I'm relieved to find somebody my own age," Rachel said. "Usually the tourists are a bunch of old-timers who bum around the country looking for clean bathrooms." Everyone laughed.

"Do you think the professor makes any sense?" Mr. Franklin asked the superintendent.

"Well, I don't know. I don't believe the cannibalism part, and the blood-filled magic bowl sounds a little far-fetched to me, but there are stranger stories in the Southwest. We're still talking more than three hundred years ago, and I don't think any of us knows all the details of what life was like back then. What I'm more worried about is the stirring-up of feelings.

"This area may have started with separate races, but after three centuries and maybe, what—fifteen generations?—everybody's family tree is mixed, with Spanish ancestors married to Puebloan ancestors and the like. Around here, marriages between races means there are families descended from both the conquered and the conquerors, and everybody's ancestors have been, at one time or another, both the abused and the abusers. There's a natural tension, but people have learned to live with it.

"People ought to be proud that their cultural heritage includes people from different backgrounds and influences. But when someone gets to thinking that their culture is being put down by someone else's, a lot of emotions rise to the surface. And if someone stirs the pot in a big way—like claiming that one group was routinely murdering another group and then eating them—it could boil over pretty easily, and we're all in trouble."

Mogi was half-listening to what his dad and Mr. Toffler were discussing. He was more interested in the gorgeous girl across from him.

He was only fourteen, looked older, and was tall for his age, but his muscles had not yet caught up with his bones, so he was gangly and spindly and a little awkward, which is to say, normal for his position in life. Taking after both his mom and his dad, he was way smarter than most of his peer group. Quick-minded, mentally disciplined, and orderly, he had a natural talent for being brainy, which seemed to earn him zero points with the opposite sex; girls seemed totally uninterested in him.

As much as he wished that things were different, he had to accept that he'd have a better time if he paid attention to other things, like the professor's mystery.

CHAPTER

3

During breakfast the next morning, a black Chevy Blazer drove into the monument campground and pulled up outside the Franklins' travel trailer. Rachel Toffler slid from the tall seat and walked toward the door, her mass of blond hair tied in a loose ponytail.

"I'm going to be your tour guide this morning for a hike into the lava fields to see the lava tubes," she announced. "I'm not actually a ranger, but they let me do the tours so I'll quit bothering them at headquarters. I'm only kidding," she laughed, "but I do love to go out into the tubes and show people around."

Having been invited for breakfast, Rachel seemed to feel instantly at ease with the family.

"Uh. . .I read a little about them but I'm still not quite sure what a, uh, lava tube is," Mogi said, struggling to sound inquisitive but not stupid. He actually knew very little about lava tubes.

"You'll understand them better when you see them," Rachel said. "Just imagine that you've got this volcano oozing lots of red-hot lava out onto the ground. But it's oozing the lava real slow, so the farther away from the mouth of the volcano the lava gets, the thicker it gets. It can be a hundred feet thick, so we're talking a lot of lava.

"When the flow slows even more, it divides into big channels and spreads out, looking like the roots of a tree. Now, for each channel, the bottom of the flow cools down, since it's against the cool ground, and the sides and top of the lava cool down, since they're exposed to the cool air.

"Eventually, as the whole flow keeps getting slower, the bottom, sides, and top become kind of solid and eventually make a thick crust. But the inside part is still really hot and keeps on flowing at a fast rate.

"The bottom, sides and top keep hardening up, and now that whole channel acts like a pipe, and the molten lava inside acts like a liquid in the pipe. When the volcano stops oozing the lava, the hot lava in the center of the pipe pulls the lava behind it, like when you suck on a straw, creating an empty space behind it after a while, and—tah dah!—a long, narrow, empty tube is left behind.

"A few hundred years later, the tubes are like really long caves. One of the tubes is seventeen miles long but has collapsed in a few places, and that's where we climb down and explore the inside.

"Now, as I tell all my visitors, these aren't caves in the usual sense because they're not *in* the ground. They're *on top* of the ground."

She smiled at Mogi. "Does that help?"

"Sure. Thanks," Mogi replied. He could have kissed her feet for just talking to him.

The official tour began at nine o'clock. An hour or so before, Jennifer and Mogi joined Rachel in her Blazer, and their parents followed in the family pickup. A few miles south of town, they pulled into the Information Center. The Franklins wandered up and down the bookshelves while Rachel and a ranger loaded the Blazer with equipment.

From the Information Center, leaving civilization behind for dirt roads, Rachel led them deeper into the rough backcountry of El Malpais and eventually pulled into a clearing next to a lava flow. Several cars were already parked in the clearing, with people putting on boots and hats.

The lava looked like a long wall of lumpy black mud that had dried in mid-squash, ten to twenty feet high. True to what Rachel had said, the huge blob lay on top of the grass as if a giant container had squeezed out a long ribbon of thick mud onto the ground.

Jennifer ran her hand over the surface.

"Good grief, this is as hard as concrete."

Mogi scanned the surface of the bulging mass. "It's all cracked and scalloped like chunks of cooled glass. Look at the crevices. I bet it's murder to walk across. No wonder the guidebook said to wear hard-soled boots if you went hiking."

Next to the glassy portion, part of the flow had a crumbly appearance, but a simple touch revealed the same hardness. Black or dark chocolate brown, the surface was mottled with different colors of sand and dirt that had blown in over the centuries. Larger, flatter surfaces were covered by the greens, grays, and reds of lichen.

"I found something on Google that said there're hardly any trails going across the lava," Mogi said. "The surface was so hard and sharp that animals couldn't travel across it, and it tore shoes and boots to shreds in no time. Travelers learned to avoid the whole area."

"That's right," Rachel said, gathering the tour group and passed out hard hats and flashlights. Rachel had a much larger light attached to her helmet, with a wire leading to a large battery on her belt. Everyone had been cautioned to wear long pants and tough hiking boots, and to carry water and a jacket.

"You want to leave your cellphones here, or at least turn them off, unless you're taking pictures. There's no cell service out here and people complain about their batteries running down because their phone is searching all the time. The biggest danger is accidentally dropping them into a crack. These rocks look solid, but they were very liquid when they flowed. When lava cools, it's like when mud dries—the surface shrinks and forms lots of cracks. Some of the cracks that we'll be stepping over today go down ten or twelve feet, and if you drop something into them, you'll never see it again."

With Rachel in the lead, the group angled across and up the crumbly bulge of rock and made their way to the top of the lava field. Once there, nothing but lava could be seen for hundreds of yards. Rachel explained about the creation of the lava beds, the different flows found around the park and their time periods, and the lava tubes.

The lava itself was so hard that despite all the walking tours that had traveled the same route, there was no worn path to follow—the lava had refused to wear away. This left the surface in its original condition—uneven, unbroken, and sharp on its edges, making each step tilted or crooked. It was hard walking.

Mogi pulled out his phone and found the photo he took during the professor's talk.

It was in the land of hard-walking.

Into the Womb of the Mother was the blood holder placed, beneath the hill in the middle of the land of hard-walking. In my dreams do I see the opening of the Womb and smell the thick smell of the river.

The land of hard-walking had to be the lava flows! Looking across to the horizon, he could see lava spreading out to the foot of the mesas miles in the distance. Against the sea of black and brown, other colors dotted the flow—the greens and grays of sagebrush, the brilliant yellow of sunflowers, the greens, browns, and muted yellows of yucca, tall grasses, and trees. Ups and downs created wave after wave of hardened lava, crevices, cracks, and caves.

This would be a great place to hide things!

The group zigzagged up a ridge and looked down into a deep, football-field-sized depression full of boulders, with a large cave opening across from them.

"This whole area is where the ceiling of a lava tube collapsed," Rachel explained. "The tube continues on both sides. We're going into that opening over there. The rocks we'll walk on to get over there were once part of the tube's ceiling."

Threading their way down a narrow line of boulders, the group walked to the bottom of the depression and crossed a field filled with large chunks of black rock, gathering just inside the cave opening. The shape of the opening was like a squashed oval, drooping in the middle and sagging at the sides. The ceiling was at least seventy-five feet above their heads.

"This is incredible. I didn't imagine it would be this big," Jennifer said to Mogi. "I bet you could park a jumbo jet in here."

One by one, walking in single file and carefully using their hands to balance on the bigger boulders, the group snaked from the opening back into the tube. Walking inside was like it had been outside, but the broken pieces of lava were larger and more angular. It took a lot of maneuvering to find a way through, and the farther they went, the darker it became.

Rachel stopped and waited for everyone to catch up.

"Lava is a very interesting rock, with some fascinating properties," she said. "As you might have noticed, it's getting dark. Even though we're only a hundred feet from the opening, there's a whole lot less light. That's because the surface of the lava is so rough that it doesn't reflect light, so any direct sunlight dies out real quick.

"So, if we move a little farther up," she said as she guided people a few more feet, down and around a few boulders, "and you turn off your lights," she spoke as she turned off her headlamp, "you begin to understand exactly what darkness is all about."

When the last light went off, there were several gasps and laughs. Mogi could not see his hand in front of his face. He had never experienced darkness so deep. He shifted his weight for a moment and suddenly felt unsteady.

"How was that for being on the dark side?" Rachel laughed as she switched her light back on. "You might have noticed that without some kind of visual reference for your eyes, and not having had time to get used to it, you can easily lose your balance. That is, you feel like you're losing your balance when, in fact, you're not even moving. I had a lady actually fall over last year, so we don't leave the lights off for long.

"Another feature you've probably also noticed," she continued, "is that lava is a fantastic insulator. I didn't have to tell most of you to put your jackets on. It's cold inside the lava tubes because cold air comes in during the winter and gets trapped. The lava then keeps it cold.

"There's a lava tube near here that's almost vertical. When rain falls through the opening, it goes all the way to the bottom where it collects in a pool. During the winters, the cold air settles into the tube and freezes the water. Because it's so well insulated, the ice hasn't melted for hundreds of years. It's a pretty cool sight. Go see it if you have the chance."

With flashlights on, the group continued forward, the many beams sweeping around the walls of the tube. Rachel spoke of the animal and insect life in the tubes and the different ecological zones they contained. They rounded a corner and were surprised by a stream of light, a few yards in diameter, which entered the tube through a single hole in the roof. The group naturally gravitated into the sunshine.

Directly below the opening, a thick layer of deep, forest-green moss and speckled lichen covered the rocks, having grown from the sunlight and rainwater that entered from the opening above. Delicate yellow and blue flowers grew in the self-made soil.

Suddenly, something shot through the opening, and a man jumped back as if a ceiling rock had fallen at his feet. Thick, gray smoke poured from the object. Mogi was startled, but curious enough to go closer.

Someone had thrown a smoke bomb through the hole!

The group broke away from the smoke, shouting in surprise.

"This way, please!" Rachel called, attempting to gather the group and direct them back through the tunnel from the direction they'd come. The smoke was quickly filling the area.

Mogi looked up and calculated that the ceiling opening was about thirty feet above him. Pulling out his handkerchief, he covered his mouth and nose, got as low as he could to the floor, and quickly made his way to the smoke bomb. It was about the size of a soup can, with smoke spewing from one end, the type he'd seen in Army surplus stores. How to pick it up? He knew it would be too hot to touch.

Mogi took off his hard hat and used a rock to nudge the smoke bomb into it. He threaded his handkerchief through the hat's straps, creating a sling, and started swinging the helmet bomb with his arm extended.

Swinging with powerful strokes, he knew he'd have to hit the opening on the first try. Feeling his muscles pull at the moment his swing arched below him and began to rise, he let go of the helmet. The smoking helmet passed through the center of the hole.

Mogi watched as it pitched over the edge, but the smoke stung his eyes and he coughed several times. His eyes filled with tears as he leaned over onto the black rocks.

Someone grabbed his shoulder. "Good shot, son!" his dad exclaimed. "That was not an easy thing to do!"

"Thanks," Mogi replied. "How come I'm not that good with a basketball?"

They worked their way over to the group, staying low to avoid the worst of the smoke. Since the opening in the ceiling was also an exit for air moving in the tunnel, the smoke cleared after a few moments.

Rachel was deep-down angry at the prank, but she paused long enough to give Mogi a deep-down admiring look and a hug. "If you hadn't done that, we could have been in real trouble," she said, reaching up to give him a kiss. The rest of the group gave him a round of applause.

Mogi was glad the light was dim—he felt like his face was glowing red.

Jennifer came up behind him and gave him a hug. "Nice work," she said, and then pointed toward Rachel, who was checking in with the other tour members. "She's pretty, huh? She's a little old for you, but it's not a bad start."

He laughed. "Oh, sure. You think she's got a little sister?"

With the assumption of there being no more smoke bombs, the group moved back into the rays of light as the final wisps of smoke floated through the opening. They hiked past the flowers of the tiny oasis and continued into the tunnel. A different light grew in front of them as they crept forward, and they soon climbed out into the bright sunshine of another caved-in portion of the tube.

A short hike up a steep slope and they were back on top of the flow, about two hundred feet from their cars. As the visitors snaked their way back to their cars, Rachel walked back and retrieved the melted lump of plastic that had been Mogi's helmet.

"I want to apologize about the smoke bomb," Rachel said as she gathered the group together to finish the tour. "We have a few teen-agers around here who think this sort of stuff is funny."

She was still angry, but contained it well, apologizing to the group and inviting them back. She cordially waved to the people as they left, but as she turned to face the Franklins, her expression shifted to one of cold, dark resentment.

"I'm going to wring his neck!" Rachel spat as she slammed the door of the Blazer. Mogi was already in the back seat and Jennifer in the front.

"Do you know who did it?" Jennifer asked.

"Oh, yeah, I know, without a doubt. We have a town jerk that is dedicated to giving me grief. He's got a chip on his shoulder the size of a boulder and is setting records for being a creep."

Mogi's mom invited Rachel to the Franklin trailer for lunch and the family soon got her back into a good mood by swapping stories and asking questions about life in a park-ranger family.

Rachel was a lot like her dad—loving the wildness of the land wherever they were and having a spirit of adventure that was never satisfied. They were always looking to find out what was beyond the next mountain, the next bend in the trail. But Rachel's mom wasn't like that, and when Mr. Toffler accepted a promotion to superintendent and transferred to El Malpais, the couple divorced. Rachel had lived with her dad most of the year from the time she was twelve and then stayed with him full-time after she graduated from high school.

Mogi and Jennifer shared stories about life in Bluff, Utah, their hometown—bare rock, canyon country on the banks of the San Juan River.

Jennifer was seventeen, three years older than Mogi. Shorter than her brother by a half-foot, with thick, brown hair cut short, she was strong, athletic, and physically graceful. She had keen "emotional radar" and loved being around people. While Mogi was the obsessive, analytical, adventurous problem-solver, Jennifer was the cautious, emotionally-centered people person. He pushed her to do more than she thought she could; she pulled him back into what was reasonable.

Both of them had great Franklin smiles.

"So, you guys are here for a couple of days and then you're going to Albuquerque," Rachel said. "I think it would be great if you hung around here longer. I mean, what does Albuquerque have that Bluff doesn't? Besides, there are so many special things to see here. The pueblos are worth visiting, and there may even be a ceremony that we could get into.

"I have an idea," she said, talking to Mogi's mom and dad, her mouth spreading into a grin. "I've got a deal going with the old pueblo at Acoma where they let me show some of my special friends around. All the ordinary tourists have to be guided by a member of the tribe, and they don't let people wander off on their own. However, me being sort of connected to the economy and having gone to school with a lot of the Acoma kids, they let me wander around on my own.

"How about this: You let me give the whole Franklin family a personalized tour of Acoma this afternoon—it's a place you don't want to miss, anyway—and then you two take off for Albuquerque tomorrow. You spend a couple of grown-up days there while Jennifer and Mogi stay here. They can stay in the trailer, and my Dad and I will be their personal guides to the Land of Enchantment."

Rachel delivered her plan with such brightness and assurance that the offer couldn't be refused. Their parents quickly warmed to the idea of having some kid-free time in the big city, and Jennifer and Mogi were excited to spend more time with Rachel.

And Mogi was thinking about the land of hard-walking and what kind of secrets it might reveal.

CHAPTER

"There's a front coming in, so it might rain, but we'll try it anyway," Rachel said as she wheeled the Blazer into the Sky City Cultural Center parking lot. "This place is way too good to pass up."

As Mogi stepped down from the back seat, he looked up at the huge mesa before him. Solid sandstone from one end to the other, towering about four hundred feet above the valley floor, it stood apart from the other mesas around it. Its weathered, creamy-white sides had been so carved by the wind that the mesa appeared to be a solid wall of massive pillars.

"The old village covers the entire flat top of the mesa," Rachel said in her tour voice. "Today, only twelve to fifteen families live full-time in the old village itself, but it used to support several hundred people."

Rachel herded the Franklins onto a small bus and spoke to them quietly as the bus started its route. "We'll stick with the regular group, and then I'll take you around to places not on the tour."

The tour guide, a young man, stood at the front of the bus and spoke to the guests.

"Welcome to Acoma Sky City Pueblo. We are the oldest continuously inhabited city in the United States and still have people who live their daily lives on top of the mesa. There's no electricity, no water system, and no sewer system. People use bottled propane for fire and light. There's no pavement on the streets because the streets are solid rock. There's no soil or vegetation, save one lonesome tree that grows next to a depression that catches rainwater. All the farming and raising of livestock are done in the valley. Before we put the road in, people climbed up and down every day to get their business done.

"For hundreds of years, the Pueblo could be reached only by a series of steps, footholds, and handholds cut into the rock in a narrow crevice that reaches all the way from the valley floor. You will have an opportunity to climb down that ancient pathway, if you wish, at the end of the tour. In the 1950s, a Hollywood movie producer built a road to the top so they could shoot a movie.

"There's not enough room on top to park many cars, so that's why we use a bus to ferry visitors from the Cultural Center."

The bus made two wide turns and then chugged up a long slope, finally stopping with a squeal and a jerk in front of a dull brown building.

Stepping from the bus, Mogi and Jennifer looked down a street, although the word "street" seemed a poor word for it. It looked more like a slightly tilted rock shelf, with the small apartment-style houses staggered along each side. The colors of the houses varied from the medium browns of adobe brick and mortar to dark adobe plaster mixed with pieces of blond straw. Several were crafted from layers of flat rock, adding texture to the earth tones. Tall log ladders, painted white, leaned against some of the houses, and black stovepipes jutted from their roofs. A few doors and window frames were painted turquoise.

To the north, a second street led to a row of houses built closer to the edge of the mesa; to the south, an open area led to buildings connected to the Acoma church, a small plaza, and a cemetery.

Mogi walked to the edge of the mesa, a hundred feet or so from the bus, and stood close to where the rock street became a cliff. The Cultural Center appeared far below. On the horizon was the dark green profile of Mount Taylor—a high, solitary mountain that served as a landmark for a hundred miles around. In front of him, to his left, to his right, above him, and below him was open space. Huge, dark-bottomed clouds hovered on the horizon in almost every direction, giving the sky a three-dimensional texture and bringing a strong updraft off the mesa wall directly into his face. Mogi closed his eyes, focused on his feet, and slowly raised his arms straight out from his sides. Then he opened his eyes, keeping them above the horizon, slightly moving his arms up and down with the wind.

He was surrounded by nature, wrapped in land and air, cradled in clouds.

"No wonder the Acoma people feel completely part of what surrounds them," Mogi said to his mom when he rejoined the family. "It's almost literally true. This isn't like being on a mountain top or anything—it's more like being suspended between earth and sky. The sky is as much a part of the surroundings as is the ground."

His mother smiled and gave his hand a squeeze.

Rachel herded the Franklins along as the tour group walked around the reception building toward the cemetery and the church.

The mission church, San Estevan del Rey, was on the south side of the village and included the huge chapel plus a square of rooms reserved for the priests and attendants. The tour guide told the history of the church while still outside, preferring to leave the inside of the church quiet. No photography was allowed.

Passing through tall, thick, rough-hewn doors with wooden hinges, the inside was a single room, long and rectangular, with a side door that led to the priest's quarters.

Mogi felt humbled. The ceiling was a good forty feet high, the room a hundred feet long and maybe forty feet wide. The floor was adobe mud on top of solid rock, worn back into dust by the many feet that had shuffled through. Only a dim glow of light came from the front door and a single window high on one wall.

Other than the ornately carved altar pieces in front and a few old pews, the inside of the church was barren of furniture.

Looking overhead, Mogi was amazed to see that the forty-foot ceiling was supported by logs that spanned the opening between the walls.

"There must be forty or fifty logs up there," Mogi whispered in wonder.

"The building of the church may have been started as early as 1630," Rachel said in a low voice as the Franklin family kept within earshot of her. "Even though priests came with Coronado in the mid-1500s, the real emphasis on establishing settlements and converting the Indians came in the late 1500s. The missionaries came to each pueblo, forced the Indians to build a mission church, and then used it for converting them to Christianity."

Pointing upward, she continued. "The logs for the ceiling came from Mount Taylor, about forty-five miles away. They were carried on the shoulders of the villagers from there to here, the priests forcing the men of the tribe to do the work.

"The logs directly above the altar were considered part of the altar, which was considered holy. Because of that, those logs were not allowed to touch the ground while they were moved, reflecting the holiness of the altar when they were put in place. If the log was set down or dropped as it was being brought here, the Indians were punished and forced to get a new one."

Mogi shook his head in wonder. How did they ever carry logs that big for all those miles? How did they ever get them up the cliffs without touching the ground?

Quietly walking the length of the long room and stepping up to the railing in front of the altar, Jennifer studied the framed paintings hung on the walls. Placards below them recounted their histories. One painting was hundreds of years old and used buffalo hide as the canvas. One very large painting was sent to the mission by the king of Spain around 1710. It had been hanging in the church for three hundred years.

"This pueblo, in particular, has terrible legacies from the conquistadors," Rachel said quietly to the Franklin family. "The most well-known is the encounter they had with Juan de Oñate, the colonizer of Nuevo Mexico who came in 1598. In response to what he understood to be a deliberate ambush of one of his nephews and ten other soldiers by a small group of Acoma men, he sent the nephew's brother to demand the pueblo's surrender so that they could be punished for the deaths.

"The pueblo leaders refused to surrender. It took a three-day battle, leaving about fourteen hundred Acoma dead and the whole pueblo burned before the chief surrendered. There was a trial for the remaining six hundred men, women, and children.

"Oñate himself was the judge. The sentence for the twenty-four men who were over twenty-five years of age was to have one foot cut off and to serve as slaves for twenty years. The other men were condemned to slavery for twenty years. The women were sentenced to slavery for twenty years, and girls twelve and younger were distributed to Spanish convents. Boys twelve and younger were given to Oñate's nephew, which meant that they were probably sold as household servants, some in Mexico.

"In one fell swoop, almost all the people of the Acoma Pueblo were enslaved, handicapped, or destroyed. It would take generations before Acoma recovered."

Jennifer looked at Rachel.

"Things like that," Jennifer said in a hushed voice, "can live in memory for a long time. No wonder there have been such hard feelings between the different cultures in New Mexico. It's obvious why your dad was concerned over that professor stirring up bad feelings."

"You don't know the half of it," Rachel replied. "There's a big monument to Oñate between Santa Fe and Taos, close to the site of the main outpost established by Oñate where he first established a permanent camp. Someone broke into the monument grounds and vandalized a bronze statue of Oñate. Want to guess what they did?"

Jennifer shook her head.

"They used an electric saw to cut off one of the statue's feet. It was never found, and they finally had the artist cast a new foot and weld it back on.

"That was in 1998, *four hundred years* after it happened." She sighed and finally said, "Well, enough of sticking with the tour group. There's a lot to see. Let me introduce you to a friend."

CHAPTER

5

As the five adventurers left the church and walked down a winding passageway between buildings, a blast of wind bowled over them with a stinging spray of dirt and sand. A sudden shadow fell around them as a huge thunderhead rolled overhead. From the dark billows of its bottom, Mogi could see a wall of rain slowly engulf the mesa.

"Uh-oh," Rachel said with a look of sudden comprehension. She started hurrying up the street, and the Franklins followed.

She passed several houses, hesitated at a couple more, and then stopped in front of a turquoise-colored doorway. As she stepped back and looked it over, confirming that it was the right house, a few small drops of rain hit the street. Within seconds, the raindrops grew larger, and then the clouds let loose.

Rachel pounded on the door. After a few seconds, the door opened and the splattered visitors dashed into the house. An native woman greeted them with a big smile.

"Rachel! Did you bring the rain with you?"

Rachel laughed. "Hi, Mrs. Abeyta! Yes, I thought I'd bring something to wet down the Acoma streets!" Everyone laughed.

The lack of sunlight outside made the inside of the home dim although a couple of propane-fed lanterns created some light. A young woman came into the room, gave Rachel a big hug, and handed towels to the visitors.

"Hey, girl," she said to Rachel.

"This is Liz," Rachel said, introducing her to the Franklins. "Liz and I played on the same softball team last year, and she is one terrific pitcher."

"Oh, I'm a great pitcher only because I hate to chase balls. I leave running after them to Rachel," Liz laughed in reply.

As everyone moved into the living room, Mogi had to smile. Being used to beige carpet, uniform white walls, electric lights, windows, curtains, furniture, electronics, and large rooms, he was fascinated by the irregularly plastered walls, intricately woven blankets and rugs on top of cement floors, wood stove, propane lights, and low ceiling with wooden beams. He and his dad had to bend over to pass through doorways.

There were a number of art pieces around the room. That is, to Mogi they were art pieces. To the Abeytas, they were everyday things—pottery, picture frames, baskets, and wood carvings. In one corner was a work table holding several pieces of unfinished clay bowls. It was obvious that, common to Puebloans and central to their heritage, the Abeyta family were potters.

The conversation was lively. Mrs. Abeyta knew her original Acoma language, Keresan, and also spoke Spanish and English. Liz knew English quite well, Spanish about half as much, and enough Keresan to understand her mother.

Jennifer and Mrs. Franklin asked the most questions, and Mrs. Abeyta was quite happy to tell about herself. She was born at the pueblo and had lived there off and on throughout her life. She had attended an Indian school growing up, plus a community college, while her children had attended school in the Acoma/Laguna district. Being the youngest daughter in the family, the family property had passed to her, and she kept the Acoma home even when she had lived elsewhere.

It wasn't long before Mrs. Abeyta was serving fresh-baked apple and cherry turnovers that she made to sell to people on the tours.

"These are wonderful," Mogi said as he started on his second one. Not small and dry like store bought ones, these turnovers were filled with fresh fruit and baked in a wood stove. The flavor was rich and full, and the unusually soft crust melted in his mouth.

In the midst of the snack, the front door opened and an elderly man walked in. The gentleman had a thick blanket draped over his head to block the rain.

Mrs. Abeyta brought him into the room and introduced him as Pablo Aguilar, her grandfather and Liz's great-grandfather. This was quite an honor for the gathering, and he soon became the center of attention.

Mogi recognized him as someone who had been at the professor's talk. Mogi couldn't hold himself back.

"You were at the talk last night," he said to the man. "What did you think of the professor?"

There was tiredness in the man's eyes as he quietly formulated his response: "The guy's an idiot."

Mogi laughed. His dad leaned forward and asked the older man if the history of the Acoma people included the story of the slave and the secret object, or the riddle describing where it was hidden.

The elderly man thought for a while and seemed to be warmed by his memories.

"The Womb of the Mother was interesting," he answered. "I don't remember any words in our chants or songs that refer to a mother's womb. We do have words that refer to sacred places and secret places, but none connected to the lava beds." He spoke in his native language to Mrs. Abeyta. She responded, shook her head a couple of times, and then shrugged her shoulders.

"As for a bowl for holding blood," he continued, "there's nothing connected to humans. We use bowls and pitchers to gather blood when we butcher pigs or goats, but it's mixed with meat to make sausage or sometimes added to a clay mixture to make floors."

He shrugged.

There were more questions about the mystery, especially from Mogi, who obviously wanted more answers than existed. The conversation turned toward life in the pueblo. Mrs. Abeyta was proud of her heritage. She enjoyed telling how the Acoma culture was directly tied to the soil, to the sky, to the valleys and mesas. Her guests were happy to listen.

"Why don't I take you around the mesa and show the place off?" Liz asked.

Everyone agreed that would be a treat. Saying thank you and good-bye to Mrs. Abeyta and her grandfather, Mogi and his family moved into the street to find that the rain had been replaced with a fine mist that swirled in and around the buildings. The sun peeked through a break in the clouds, and strong rays of light lit them from beneath, turning them a blush red. A soft, glowing, indirect light tinged with pink enveloped the ancient community.

Mogi was impressed and barely refrained from taking pictures, since he had not paid the camera fee. Acoma took on a completely different feeling when it was wet from rain. In place of the drab variations of brown, the sandstone had a richer hue, and the adobe finishes on the buildings shone with a burnished bronze in the reflected sunlight. The rock surface of the streets was shiny with wet reflections; each small puddle became a mirror.

It reminded Mogi of his own special place. Far up one of the canyons behind his house in Bluff, Mogi had discovered an Anasazi ruin high in a cliff above the canyon floor. He knew of no one who had been there. It was a place he went when he needed to be alone.

In the back of the ruin, a small opening led into a narrow crevice in the rock. Years of erosion had given the crevice a flat floor of sand and, as he sat on the floor, he was fully surrounded by towering walls of sandstone. Mogi would sit and listen to the sounds echoing in the crevice. He knew the sounds were caused by wind and rock, but it was fun to pretend that he was hearing the voices of the ancient Anasazi, whispering secrets.

He caught up with Liz, Rachel, and the others at the edge of the mesa and looked across the valley below.

Special places, he thought, as he was awed by the miles and miles of open country. How many people in history had special places they were willing to die for?

Liz led them around the different streets, into the ceremonial plaza, and back to the cemetery next to the mission church. As she did, she told more of the stories of Acoma, its history, and how its people lived today.

Reluctantly, Rachel announced it was time to go. The guests expressed their appreciation to Liz for the tour and her family's hospitality and said goodbye. Rachel led the Franklins across the street and to the edge of a cliff close to the road that brought the tour bus.

"This is the fun part," Rachel said as she moved to the left of the edge, stepped onto the lower rocks, and then descended into a small crevice in the mesa rim. Mogi and his sister followed, their parents behind. They were descending the famous stairway, a narrow and twisting series of steps and handholds leading to the valley hundreds of feet below.

How many times has this been traveled, Mogi wondered, as he balanced in the steep footholds, now not much more than shallow depressions in the rock surface. Holding securely to well-worn handholds on each side, he kept putting one foot below the other, following Rachel until the steps ran out on a small hill next to the road.

CHAPTER 6

The Franklins invited Rachel and her dad to their trailer for dinner that evening. It was an offer enthusiastically accepted."

"So, you never told us about the smoke bomb guy," Jennifer said to Rachel after they had filled their plates with hamburgers.

"It's not much of a story," Rachel began as she passed the ketchup. "Manuelito Alfonso Garcia is the town jerk. He was in school for a long time, being as he had a problem graduating. He finally got old enough to quit, but he still hangs out at school. I graduated in May and thought I was done with him."

"Does he live close to you? Why does he pick on you?" Jennifer couldn't help being curious.

"I have no idea where he lives and I don't know why he's decided to make me the object of his attention. Maybe nobody else will put up with him.

"His basic problem is that his dad is from northern Mexico and his mother is from Acoma. I don't know how they met. His grandmother actually lives in Sky City, in one of the apartments on the mesa. The result is that he doesn't fit into the native culture since he's not considered a true-enough Puebloan, and the Hispanic community doesn't accept him because they don't regard Mexicans all that highly.

"It's a common story— a teen-ager with a muddled heritage in a community where heritage really matters. I might feel sorry for him if he didn't act like such a jerk. Mixed ancestry isn't an excuse for bad behavior."

"I'm sure he isn't welcome in the Anglo community, either," Mr. Toffler began. "In 1950, a Navajo sheepherder by the name of Paddy Martinez discovered a uranium deposit north of the city. That led to the discovery that New Mexico has the second-largest identified uranium ore reserves in the United States, and most of it is directly north of Grants. That got a lot of big companies excited, and all sorts of people moved in. The mines increased the number of Anglos, which reinforced a group that is used to dominating.

"And if that weren't enough," he continued, "it also divided people along economic lines: those whose economy was industry-based, such as the geologists, miners, and engineers, and those who based their lives on farming, ranching, and crafts, such as the Puebloans and Hispanics. It was the haves and the have-nots, which implied that heritage and tradition weren't as valued as knowledge and education.

"Then you add archaeologists, sociologists, and others like our good professor the anthropologist, and suddenly cultural identity is touted as a national treasure. I'm sure everybody meant well, but it has just increased the number of ways that people had to compete."

"I wish the audience had been more interested in the slave's story rather than the professor's conclusion," Mogi said. "Of course, he didn't give them much of a chance."

Mr. Toffler finished the last bite of his hamburger. "By the way, I asked Dr. Chandler about the river that was mentioned in the riddle, and he didn't have a clue what it referred to. The 'land of hard-walking' is a name the pueblos used for the lava beds, which is why he's getting permission for his research through the political channels of the monument. I asked him if he had any additional leads, but apparently the document and its riddle are all there is. At least, that's all that he was willing to say. I'm pretty sure he wouldn't tell me if there were more. He doesn't seem like the type to share secrets."

*   *   *

Rachel arrived at the trailer in the morning with a story to tell.

"Well, there's good news and there's bad news," she began as she sat down at the breakfast table. "Somebody sliced all of Dr. Chandler's tires last night outside his motel room. He's throwing a fit about it. He got my dad out of bed to rant about it, but my dad couldn't do anything. He finally offered him a Park Service pickup while his car gets new tires. I think my dad is counting the days until this geek finally leaves.

"The good news, however," Rachel continued, "is that Mrs. Abeyta sent Liz into town last night to leave a message for us. Her father remembered something more about the professor's story and thought we would be interested. He would like for us to come back. He's especially interested in talking to the young man who asked all the questions," she said as she smiled at Mogi.

"Hey, my kind of guy," Mogi said.

As Mr. and Mrs. Franklin left for their side trip to Albuquerque, the teens made plans to return to Acoma Pueblo.

"How about some coffee before we set out?" Rachel asked. Mogi didn't drink coffee, but Jennifer enjoyed visiting cafes in the various towns they visited. In Grants, that meant the McDonald's, and that was their first stop.

A few minutes after they sat down in a booth, a 1965 Chevy Bel Air lurched into the lot and parked next to the Blazer. It sported various colors of metal primer—gray, red, and a few white patches.

"Oh, no," Rachel moaned as Manuelito Alfonso Garcia entered the restaurant in his headband and dark sunglasses. He looked over and smiled.

"Hey, white girl, you miss me?" he called, heading toward the counter.

Rachel jumped out of her seat and marched toward the boy. Mogi thought she was going to take his head off.

"You creep!" she hissed. "Don't you know people can get hurt in the tubes if they can't see? Don't you ever do that again! Why won't you leave me alone?"

The boy grinned, shrugged his shoulders, and made some slinky moves with his arms. "I was just helping you out, girl. You need a little adventure with your honky tourists," he said.

As the boy's face lit up with a show of white teeth, Mogi recognized him as the guy Rachel slapped at the professor's presentation. The headband was unmistakable, and Mogi remembered his grin and the way he moved his hands.

Jennifer got up and joined Rachel.

"Hi! I'm Jennifer Franklin," she said brightly, reaching out her hand for a handshake.

The boy was taken aback but regained his composure enough to ignore her hand.

"I hear you're one of the outstanding citizens of this wonderful town," Jennifer continued with a bold voice, again with an outstretched hand and a bright smile, not accepting the boy's rebuff.

This time the boy actually shook her hand. "Oh, yeah, that's me, I guess, an outstanding citizen."

"Come on over and join us. We honky tourists are eager to get to know the local folks, if they're not afraid," Jennifer said.

He looked a little surprised as he moved up in the line. Once he had his food, he shuffled over to the table and sat down in the booth with Rachel, Jennifer, and Mogi. Manuelito was clearly uncomfortable. He was not as tall as Mogi, but he had developed muscles, a grown man's face, and coal-black hair combed straight back under the bandanna. Mogi guessed he was about twenty.

Jennifer asked questions about his car, his job, his family, and a dozen other topics, all of which earned her a few short answers. It wasn't long before—at least for a moment—he seemed like an ordinary young man.

Mogi focused on his second breakfast, a double order of fries, drowning them in ketchup. Rachel drank her coffee.

"Oh, I have a question about the lava beds, but I need a map. Do you have a monument map in your Blazer?" Mogi asked Rachel.

"Uh, sure," she replied. The two of them got up from the booth and went outside.

"I can't believe my sister," Mogi said as they opened the Blazer and Rachel handed him the map. "Give me a good puzzle, or a riddle, or a mystery anytime, before you ask me to do social work." He smiled broadly at Rachel.

"Is that what she's doing? I couldn't figure it out. I'm hard pressed to give the jerk the time of day, much less have a conversation with him."

"Well, you have to cut Jennifer some slack. She can't help but feel for people who have troubles in life, and she connects to people even before she knows she's doing it. Fortunately, she's really good at it."

Mogi took the map and spread it out on the hood of the Blazer. "Is there a place where we can get a good look at the entire monument?" he asked. "Some place a lot higher than everything else that would let us look from one end to the other?"

Rachel started tracing her finger along the map.

"You're camped on the west side of the beds, right along here, on Highway 53. The Information Center is here. If you go to the other side of the beds," she traced the route up with her finger through Grants and then back down on the other side, "on 117, you can see these mesas to the east of the highway. The road goes right along the base of them. See the mesa tops colored differently? I'm not sure exactly who owns the land, but it may be the western boundary of the Acoma reservation.

"If you look right here," she pointed to one location, leaned her head down, and squinted at the small print, "there's a peak called North Pelon. It's not really a peak, just an outcropping on top of a big mesa. You can see it from the highway. The elevation"—she squinted at the map again—"is 8,500 feet, which is around two thousand feet above the valley floor. If you stood right there, you'd be able to see most of the monument all at once.

"I can probably get us close. We may have to walk some to get to the highest point, but I don't think it would be too hard."

"Uh, if it's not too much trouble, I'd like to go there," Mogi said. "If I could see everything, maybe I could make more sense out of the riddle. Do you think we could go today, sometime?"

Rachel thought for a moment, sorting through the list of things she had planned. "We're headed for Acoma in a minute, and that'll probably take us until noontime. We wouldn't be that far away, so we can detour up there on the way back. I'm a little puzzled what you'll get out of it, though."

Mogi smiled and shrugged his shoulders. He didn't tell her that he had no idea.

Jennifer came outside and joined them.

"So, how's our hometown jerk today?" Mogi asked with a cocky smile.

"Hey, don't be so hard on the guy. He's not so bad," she said and then added with a smile, "You'll like him. I told him you'd be happy to come down some weekend and help him paint his car."

Rachel laughed as they all climbed into the Blazer.

*   *   *

Mrs. Abeyta greeted them at the door. Her grandfather was already there, and as the three teenagers had guessed, he had been ready for some time. They sat on the rugs surrounding his chair.

He told several stories, explaining the ancient origins of the lava beds, describing the connections of the beds to the animals, insects, and people, and then mentioned some of the ways the beds figured in the Acoma religion.

"I remembered an old legend," he finally said. "The legend spoke of a hidden river in the land of hard-walking, but I didn't remember a story or song about it." He paused. "This made me curious and I went and spoke to others in the village. One remembered a story of a river that was lost, but could not remember if it was the same story as the hidden river.

"We thought for a long time and he remembered a riddle he had heard as a young man:

> *A river there is.*
> *One cannot see it, but it is there.*
> *One cannot hear it, but it talks still.*
> *One cannot touch it, but walks upon it."*

Mogi listened carefully and then typed the exact words into his phone as a text to himself. He asked some questions, but Mr. Aguilar could supply no more details.

When it seemed time, they thanked Mrs. Abeyta and her grandfather for their hospitality. It was almost noon. Liz joined them for the walk to the rock-cliff stairway. Enjoying the sunlight and the extraordinary views, they wandered through the streets, admiring the pottery and jewelry the villagers displayed on tables outside their homes.

In front of one home was an elderly Acoma woman arranging freshly baked bread on a table. Liz stopped and spoke to the woman in the Acoma language. The woman smiled with closed lips and placed a loaf of bread into a used grocery sack. As Liz paid for the bread, the elderly woman sat back in her chair in the shade of a wall. The group of teenagers moved down the street.

"I thought you might like to see her," Liz said to Rachel. "I mean, you might be related to her someday."

Rachel stared at her friend in confusion. "And just what does that mean?" she asked.

"Well," Liz started and then broke out in a broad grin, "that's Manny Garcia's grandmother, and you two have the hots for each other, I can tell."

Rachel laughed as she chased Liz through the streets. They finally stopped to catch their breath, more from laughing than exertion.

*   *   *

Mogi sat in the back seat of the Blazer, his arms folded. Hidden river. Walk on it, can't hear it, can't see it.

"So, uh, what do you think about a hidden river out in the lava beds?" he asked Rachel. "Ever seen a river out there?"

Rachel gave a little laugh.

"Let me answer you this way. One summer, I helped my dad do a computer mapping survey of El Malpais for the Bureau of Land Management. We walked over the main parts of the flows with a survey stick equipped with a GPS and put down markers at the grid points. When we were finished, they did aerial photographs, which they will repeat every couple of years or so. Using the data, they'll be able to determine if the beds are shifting and by how much.

"I can tell you that after walking miles and miles out there, there is no river. Believe me, except for what fills up with water after a rain, there's not enough water out there to fill a bucket, much less a river."

"Okay, well, given that information, we've got a real mystery then," Mogi responded. "Even if there were a river in the 1600s and it dried up, you'd be able to see the riverbed. The lava has been there for a few thousand years, so no new river has shown up.

"So, on one hand, we've got a riddle that there was a river because he smelled it, and another riddle saying there was a river, but you couldn't see it, hear it, or touch it, but could walk on top of it. Now an eyewitness swears there is definitely no river anywhere out there. I think I'm totally confused."

Rachel pointed the car toward a turnoff that would lead them high into the mesas overlooking the monument.

CHAPTER

7

"This is where we want to go," Mogi said as he leaned forward from the back seat and put his finger on the map Jennifer held. "All we have to do is find it."

For the first half hour, Rachel took the back roads on the reservation like she knew where she was going. The rain of the previous day had made the packed dirt road soft and sometimes slick. Part of the road angled across the side of a mesa as they left the valley and gained elevation. Once on top, driving became easier.

"I've been down some of these roads, but not all," Rachel said as she drove. "Acoma Pueblo, being an independent nation, gets very little road maintenance funds except for state and federal highways and roads. This means that once you get out in the boonies, a road drawn on the map may be little more than ruts."

The top of this mesa was not as barren as the solid rock of Acoma's mesa, where they'd met Liz and her family, but it was still as untouched a country as Mogi had ever seen. No buildings, no houses, no signs, no road markings, no telephone poles, no fields, no fences, no fence posts. Nothing but wide open space.

As barren as the country was back home around Bluff, there were always signs that people had been there: a network of roads, signs indicating buried pipes, or old settlements. Where they were now made Bluff look like the middle of a suburb. There was nothing here but piñon, cedar, and juniper trees, with tall grasses replacing the sage of the valley. Every now and then, a tall pine stuck out of the ground like a grave marker.

The cold front that had moved through the day before, bringing the brief thunderstorm at the pueblo, had clouded the skies and was settling again over the area. Gusty winds buffeted the Blazer while the layer of clouds and sporadic rain kept it cool. Moving into the higher country of the mesas, the clouds hung closer to the ground and added an increasing chill.

Mogi watched the clouds. The dark bottoms, with white billows on top, had now blended with other clouds, leaving a dark line above the horizon and a long gap of sunlight. Every now and then, he heard the growls of distant thunder.

Looking at the map over Jennifer's shoulder, Mogi knew they were near where they wanted to be. "We should be able to see the outcropping pretty soon," he said.

Coming over a rise, the horizon was far in the distance, so the edge of their mesa had to be close. Looking to his right, Mogi saw a rocky bump.

"I bet that's it," he said excitedly. "That must be North Pelon."

Rachel slowed down. "I don't see any road over to it, so I think we're on foot from here."

Mogi was already gathering up the daypacks.

"What about rain and lightning?" Jennifer asked.

"The thunder we've heard is pretty far away," Rachel replied. "I think we can make it over there and back no sweat. I'm glad we all brought jackets, though; it's a lot colder here than back in Sky City."

Rachel pulled the Blazer to the side of the road. Everyone hustled. The wind was gusting, whipping sprays of cold in their faces. No one talked as they bowed their heads and headed toward the edge. It was about a hundred yards to the rocky point. Walking around it, they realized there was no easy way up. "Let's take a look at the beds from the edge of the mesa!" Mogi called over the noise of the wind as he headed in that direction. "That may be all I need to get a full view." The cold was biting, and they hunkered close to each other as they came up to the edge.

The view was awesome. The guidebooks talked about the various flows in El Malpais coming from different volcanoes at different times, new flows adding layers on top of old flows. From a car, not much could be seen. From two thousand feet above, however, they could see the different lava flow's distinct shapes, textures, and colors. The more recent flows looked like islands of black in a sea of green and gray, reminding him of the harsh texture of sea coral. The older flows had varying levels of vegetation, although the presence of trees was a good indication of their ages. In the midst of one section of flow, there was a small forest of tall pines that looked healthy and happy.

Rachel pointed to the trees. "Most people consider lava as unable to support plant life, but it's only partly true," she said. "Even though it doesn't break down into conventional soil, lava is really excellent at storing water. Add a little dirt brought in by the wind, and bushes and trees can live for a long time on the water from periodic snows or rains. Some of the cedar trees out there are hundreds of years old."

Mogi took out a park map, struggled to unfold it against the wind, and finally gave up. He took the binoculars as the two girls sat down and huddled against the wind, zipping their jackets up against their chins.

Mogi knew he needed to be quick about this. The line of clouds in the distance had a curtain of rainfall hanging beneath. By watching the progress of the rain, he judged that it would be over the mesa in twenty or thirty minutes. If he had brought Jennifer and Rachel all the way out here just to get hit with a rainstorm, he'd feel pretty stupid. He hurried.

Mogi peered through the binoculars and slowly moved from one end of the monument to the other, still not sure what he was looking for. He remembered the essential elements of the document's message—some kind of bowl for holding liquids, a hill in the middle of the "land of hard-walking," and the smell of a river. Combined with the legend from Liz's great-grandfather, there must have been a river or something that could be called a river.

It suddenly occurred to him that maybe the "river" only appeared during rainstorms. He looked for how rain would have run off the land. The land sloped from west to east, from far across to right below the mesa he now sat on. That must be the Continental Divide; he had seen the dotted line on Rachel's map and remembered a road sign on the way to the lava tubes.

"Rachel, do you know of any riverbeds south of the monument?"

"I can't think of anything definite. Going south, you eventually run into the mountains above Datil. The mountains are a lot higher than here," she said, pointing to the large, shadowy outlines in the distance.

Mogi thought for a minute. "OK, has anybody ever mapped possible riverbeds underneath the lava?"

"I have no idea."

Mogi's gaze swept across the beds again and then focused on following the edges. He saw no riverbeds, no gullies or arroyos, no eroded cliffs. He glanced over at the thunderstorm. It had moved faster than he expected. The sky was getting dark enough that he could see some lights from Grants in the distance.

"It's time to get out of here, dork-boy," Jennifer said in a shivering voice. "It's going to be big-time nasty here in a minute."

Mogi wasn't finished, even though he didn't know what else he could do. Taking his phone, he took pictures from right to left across the whole monument.

A storm could mean a world of hurt out in the middle of nowhere, he thought as he unzipped his backpack and put his binoculars away. Jennifer was already trotting back to the Blazer, Rachel close behind.

They reached the SUV just in time. Before the big rain hit, strong gusts of wind rocked the Blazer back and forth. Moments later, it felt like a monstrous bucket of water had been poured on top of the vehicle.

Rachel turned the vehicle around and headed across the mesa. No one could talk over the sound of hammering rain on the roof, and soon the noise increased. The rain turned to pea-sized hail, and it wasn't long before the ground around them was covered deep enough with hail that it looked white. It looked like winter.

"This is not good!" Rachel called out over the noise. "We've seen storms put a foot or more of hail on the ground in half an hour. It'll turn the road into grease."

The Blazer slid sideways with a jerk and fishtailed in and out of a ditch of chocolate-colored slush. As Rachel straightened the vehicle, she pushed a button on the console, switching to four-wheel drive. It made driving considerably better, but the hail continued to pile up on the road.

Every depression in the road was a pit of muck. Rachel kept the front wheels turned in the direction of the road in case she slid and skillfully negotiated each dip. Topping a rise,

Rachel brought the Blazer to a stop. The road was blocked. A vehicle up ahead had slid in a dip and turned sideways. The driver was uselessly spinning the wheels, working the car deeper into the mud.

A '65 Chevy Bel Air, mostly gray-primer colored.

"Ha! Serves him right for following me this time!" Rachel cackled.

They sat for a minute.

"Do you have a chain in this buggy?" Mogi asked.

"Oh, yeah. My dad outfits our cars just like the Park Service pickups. We've got tire chains, a shovel, ropes, a long chain, and there's a towrope, too."

The hail was about two inches deep when the storm lightened to a drizzle. Rachel pulled off the road, moved around the stuck Chevy, went back onto the road, and backed up until she was as close to the car as possible without being caught in the thick mud.

Mogi crawled over the back seat, found the towrope, lifted the back window, and stepped down into a brown ooze mixed with bits of ice. He tied the rope to the trailer hitch on the Blazer and ran the length to the Bel Air, bending down far enough to securely catch the center of the front bumper. He didn't even bother talking to Manny. It wasn't like he was going to give the guy directions on how to be towed. When Mogi got back into the Blazer, his shoes were soaked.

Rachel went into low four-wheel drive for better traction and the Blazer did the rest. Once she'd pulled the Bel Air to the top of the hill, Mogi got back out, disconnected the towrope, and moved over to the car's window. It slowly cranked down.

"Follow us and we'll make sure you're OK before we get too far ahead," he told Manny, who looked embarrassed.

Whaddya know, he thought to himself. The guy doesn't look so tough when he's stuck in the mud. Why did he follow them out there, anyway? It wasn't a proper road to begin with, and with the Bel Air so low to the ground, he should have expected trouble. Was giving Rachel grief really that important? Was he as taken with her as much as Mogi was?

It was not much farther to the incline down to the valley. With better drainage and more protection from the sides of the mesa, the road was better, and they had no more problems. Finally pulling onto a paved road, Rachel shifted the Blazer back into two-wheel drive. The hail had changed to rain and was now a drizzle. When they reached the interstate, the Bel Air, having followed faithfully behind, sped up and passed them. There was no wave.

"The guy didn't even say thank you," Mogi said.

"Don't take it personally," Jennifer said. "He would if he could. He just doesn't know how."

CHAPTER

8

They stopped at a car wash on the outskirts of Grants and washed the mud off the Blazer. Mogi took off his shoes and gave them a spray as well. Rachel needed to check in with her dad, so they drove to the monument headquarters.

Pulling into the parking lot, they stared at a crowd of people in front of the building surrounding a Park Service pickup that looked like it had been through a war. The windows were smashed, the headlights were knocked out, and the fenders and doors were dented. The hood was up, showing the engine wiring in shambles. The driver's side door was spray-painted with the word "BLOOD" in large letters.

"Wow," was all Mogi managed to say.

As they cautiously entered the building, they saw the professor in the superintendent's office, furiously striding up and down and shouting at Rachel's father. The office secretary related the story to the three teens as they waited in the lobby.

Professor Chandler had been in the southwestern end of El Malpais, looking for cave openings. After he'd worked uninterrupted for about an hour, four men suddenly appeared from behind a grove of trees and started moving toward him. Having the good sense to know they weren't there to help, he took off running across the lava flow as fast as he could. They had almost caught him before they gave up and retreated.

Once he'd made it back to the pickup, the professor found it mostly destroyed. It took him an hour to hike to the Information Center, where he demanded a wrecker tow it to the monument headquarters.

The three friends listened to the yelling and shouting coming from Mr. Toffler's office. The professor was relentless in his anger. At last, he spat out a final word, strode out of the office, and banged out the front door.

Bob Toffler looked around cautiously as he came out of his office, breathing a sigh of relief. "I truly don't like that man," he said flatly.

The teens followed him into his office.

"The tire slashing last night was on the professor's car," he explained, motioning the teenagers to sit down. "That was bad enough, but this is vandalism of government property, plus attempted assault. This might get out of hand, so I have to report the incident.

"Chandler has made the pueblo mad with the cannibalism accusations, he's made the Hispanics mad because he's dragged up the old Spanish atrocities, and he's made the community of Grants mad because he's an outsider who's looking to disregard the collective honor of everyone and make them all out to be uneducated heathens."

He sighed again.

"So, that's the excitement of my day. What have you been up to?"

Mogi joined the others in relating their activities of the afternoon. What Liz's great-grandfather, Mr. Aguilar, had to say was interesting but not very enlightening. Mr. Toffler was glad they had used their heads and gotten out of the mountains when they did, and he wasn't surprised at Manny's appearance—he'd been a constant thorn in Rachel's side for the past couple of years, but seemed innocent enough. God knew there were plenty of boys attracted to his daughter. If it turned to stalking, then it would be different.

"I think this deserves supper," Mr. Toffler said. "If you'll let me finish up the report on the pickup, we'll go find some food."

Mogi thought that was a great idea—he was starving. Jennifer had asked Rachel to spend the night at the trailer, and having supper together would give them all a chance to get to know each other better.

As he waited for the superintendent to finish, Mogi looked at the photographs on the wall of the entry area and read some of the posters. Behind the receptionist's desk was a large aerial photograph of El Malpais. Mogi located the mesa they had driven to and North Pelon Point. He put his finger on where he must have stood.

Taking out his phone and turning it sideways to line up with the photograph, he compared the two. Remembering what he had seen, and drawing straight lines from his sitting point to various features across the lava flows, he found some of what he remembered—high points, the different colors of the vegetation, the different flows, the islands of barren, black lava, and the ragged edges of the beds next to the road.

After spending a few minutes up close, he backed up and leaned against the receptionist's desk, viewing the monument as a whole.

How do you hide a river?

Several minutes passed. Nothing came to him. El Malpais was one big place. The lava beds covered several square miles, having oozed in different directions at different times, and the crusty texture of the big waves of lava made unusual features hard to see. Everything looked so different that it all looked the same.

Mr. Toffler came out of his office.

"I have served my country beyond the call of duty," he said, "and it's time to eat."

He took them to a restaurant with a full salad bar and a dessert bar. It made Mogi realize how little variety of food his mom and dad had packed in the RV, and how much he really loved restaurants. It wasn't long before his salad plate was piled high.

The conversation turned to the professor's mess. It was obvious that Mr. Toffler was concerned more about the community's feelings than harboring a grudge against Dr. Chandler.

"Chandler is just another anthropologist. People around here have seen them come and go, along with the science and engineering types, and anyone else who pokes around the countryside for a living, looking either at rocks or ruins. Some day, Chandler will be gone and his ideas will fade away.

"The real problem is that bringing back the memories of abuse, hatred, injustice, and persecution rebuilds the barriers between people, and barriers based on historical events can be some of the worst."

A waiter served the entrees, and Mogi's attention shifted to his food. As Mr. Toffler talked, Mogi admired the steak before him and imagined the great taste of the mashed potatoes and gravy.

Mogi started thinking.

His mashed potatoes looked up at him. There was a pool of gravy in the middle. Taking his fork, he lifted the sides of the potatoes around the gravy and over the top. The gravy disappeared under a roof of potatoes. He remembered sitting next to Mr. Aguilar as he told the words of the riddle.

A river there is.
One cannot see it, but it is there.
One cannot hear it, but it talks still.
One cannot touch it, but walks upon it.

A hidden river. Like a hidden lake of gravy.

He had asked the wrong question when he looked at the photograph on the wall.

"Are you all right?" Jennifer asked as she leaned over. Mogi realized he had been staring at his food.

"Oops, sorry. I was just thinking."

He looked at Mr. Toffler. "Would you mind if, after we eat, we go back to the office? I want another look at the aerial photograph of the monument."

"Sure, no problem at all," Mr. Toffler responded.

With that, Mogi rejoined the group and made quick work of everything that touched his fork.

*   *   *

Professor Chandler was at the headquarters' door when they pulled up. He had just dropped an envelope through the mail slot.

"Oh, great," Bob Toffler said under his breath as they got out.

"Dr. Chandler," he said in greeting. "What can I do for you?"

"I was dropping off the receipts for my tires. I expect full reimbursement."

"Well, let's see," Mr. Toffler responded. "Seems like your car insurance should cover it. You were parked at a public motel. How do you figure that the monument should pay for your tires?"

"You're not getting out of this!" the professor yelled. "I was giving that lecture at your request, so I was here because the government asked me to be, so don't give me any bull about not being responsible!"

"So if we find your precious object, that means we get to keep it, right?"

It was Rachel. She resented her father being attacked by some slob who felt he was entitled to anything he wanted.

"What are you talking about?" the professor shot back.

"You don't know what to look for! I've spent years doing this research. You don't have a chance of finding anything."

"Oh, yeah? Stand back and watch! We know things you don't have a clue about!"

"OK, OK," Mr. Toffler said as he stepped between them. "Let's not worry about ancient objects right now, all right? We're not talking mysteries, we're talking tires."

Jennifer pulled Rachel away and led her into the building, leaving Mr. Toffler and the professor to argue.

"It just boils my blood to see a jerk like that go after the monument," Rachel continued to rail. "He should consider himself a guest, not some member of a royal family we're supposed to serve. He thinks he's entitled, but he's not."

She had a good audience, with Jennifer and Mogi rushing to give their support to her dad.

What I wouldn't give to solve this, Mogi thought. I'd love to rub that magic bowl in that guy's face.

A few minutes passed before Mr. Toffler came through the door. He stepped over the envelope on the floor with Professor Chandler's receipt for the tires.

"He can leave me anything he wants," Mr. Toffler said with a smile, "but he can't make me pick it up. It'll wait until tomorrow."

The four of them gathered in front of the aerial photo, and Mogi leaned against the receptionist's desk.

"I was looking at this earlier and I had one question: How do you hide a river? According to Chandler's document and the riddle from Mr. Aguilar, there was some kind of river in El Malpais. But there's one basic problem: There *is no river* in El Malpais, and it doesn't look like there's ever been one.

"So, I started thinking, suppose there was something that could be called a river in El Malpais. How could I hide it? One way would be to put it in a lava tube. Maybe a spring broke through the bottom of a tube and flowed totally within the tube. There'd be a river, but you wouldn't see it, and you could walk on top of it, just like Mr. Aguilar said. But the water would eventually run out, and you'd know it.

"A second way is to have a river that had dried up between then and now. Any river of reasonable size would leave a riverbed. But there's no sign of a riverbed.

"I thought of underground caverns, like at Carlsbad Caverns. There are underground lakes and rivers in cave networks. That's not unusual. Underground water that is a source for well water is sometimes called an 'underground river.' With our stories, though, a river that deep doesn't fit. They both seem to describe something close to the surface since it could be smelled."

The others were listening as Mogi continued.

"I realized during supper that I was asking the wrong question. It's not, How do you hide a river? The question should be, How do you see a river that's hidden? This made me think of the Great Sand Dunes Monument, up in Colorado."

"I've been there several times," Mr. Toffler said. "I bet you're thinking of the river that disappears into the sand."

"Yes sir, that's exactly what I'm thinking," Mogi replied. "The Sand Dunes River, made up of water from springs and runoff from the mountains east of the dunes, runs along the foot of the dunes. When our family camped at the Great Sand

Dunes National Monument, we played in the water, waded in it, buried our feet in it. In another mile, though, the river disappears. The soil under the dunes is really porous and soaks up every drop of water that runs onto it. But you know it's still there even a few miles later."

"The trees!" Jennifer said. "I remember the willows and cottonwoods next to the riverbed."

She spoke to Rachel and her father. "It was really apparent when we climbed to the top of a dune and looked back at the campground. The river was gone, but going into the distance for miles were trees, shrubs, and thickets, as if the river were still there."

Mogi pointed at the map.

"If there were a river out there, but we couldn't see it, how would we know it was there?"

He and the others looked up and down the aerial photograph. Something caught Mogi's eye. Along the south edge of the flows, near the southern end of the monument, one area was filled with yellows and reds. Along the other edges, the colors were very distinctive: black or dark brown where the lava was; sand-colored, green, or gray where the lava was not.

Mogi pulled out his phone and looked at his pictures. The location of the colors in the photograph on the wall had the bright green colors of summer on his phone.

"What's right here?" he asked Mr. Toffler as he pointed to the yellows and reds.

"It's a large grove of cottonwood trees, plus bunches of Gambel oaks and tamarisk. This picture was taken in October, because the cool air made for a better photograph and the trees were in the middle of turning."

He paused and thought aloud. "I've been to that place. It's like an oasis in this country. There are hardly any other cottonwoods or oaks in the entire monument. There's nothing on the surface, but it obviously has a lot of water under the surface."

He thought for a minute. "I believe you're onto something here."

Mogi looked intently at the spot on the photograph. What he was remembering, though, was the anger in the voices of the audience at the professor's talk. If that anger kept increasing, more confrontations would occur, and it wouldn't be good. People couldn't keep their anger in and eventually, somebody was going to get hurt. The mysterious grove of cottonwoods might be a clue to the mystery. Maybe, just maybe, it would lead to the discovery of the mysterious object.

But would solving a three hundred year-old mystery make the situation in town better? Or worse?

CHAPTER

Rachel and Jennifer closed their eyes as they lay back against the cushions while Mogi leaned forward and put his head on the trailer's dining table. It had been a long day, with a lot of miles covered and some tough things happening. They were content to finally be in the coziness of the trailer.

"What do we do now?" Jennifer asked. Mr. and Mrs. Franklin had left only that morning, though it seemed longer. There would still be another day and another night before they came back, and then the family would return to their vacation timetable and she'd probably never see Rachel again.

Their part in the mystery would be over. If Chandler was proved right by some means and his conclusions were true, then she wasn't sure what would happen. Maybe a civil war. But she wasn't sure who would be on which side. If it weren't solved— if the professor didn't find the proof of cannibalism—then life would go on and the people would have to handle the anger that had flared up. Maybe things would return to normal.

Either way, she and Mogi and their parents would be far down the road by that time, which would be disappointing. A newly discovered mystery that actually had been around a few hundred years was just such an entertaining idea! To have the first riddle, and then Mr. Aquilar's riddle—she wasn't any good at solving mysteries, but she could tell her brother was already on the chase.

And then there was the *need* to solve it. Whether she liked the professor or not, the sudden violence toward him was disturbing. If it got worse, then Rachel's dad was going to be sucked in even more into trying to stop it, and Rachel was going to be right there with him.

"You think we have a chance at finding something?" she said to the back of her brother's head.

Mogi's forehead was still on the table. It rolled back and forth a couple of times and then rose up to look at her. "I don't know," he said honestly.

He needed some alone time to think. Although first excited about the discovery of the cottonwood grove and its seemingly unusual growth, he now felt tired and discouraged. To consider finding a sacred object or an object of power or even an ordinary bowl, magic or not, out there in the lava flows seemed foolish. How could he have even imagined something like that?

It was impossible to answer even the simple questions: What if the sacred object had been buried? What if it had been lowered into a crevice? What if the sacred place had been in a lava tube that had since collapsed? The Womb of the Mother could have a large arrow pointing to it, painted in white, and you'd still have to wander through several square miles of brutal rock to see it.

No wonder it had never been found.

Maybe what we do now is quit, he thought. It would save more wasted effort. Tomorrow, we could play tourist at the other pueblos, go up Mount Taylor, or maybe visit the El Morro National Monument, where travelers had carved their names into the side of sandstones cliffs for hundreds of years.

Mogi lowered his head back to the table and it was still there when the three friends were surprised by the sound of a car pulling up outside the trailer. Eyes open, no one moved.

A car door opened and slammed, footsteps crunched on the gravel in front of the trailer, and there was a knock at the door. It wouldn't be Rachel's father—it hadn't been half an hour since they'd left him.

Were the bad guys now after them?

Mogi quietly slipped from behind the table and moved to the door, thankful he had locked it out of habit. Without opening the door, he called out.

"Who's there?"

There was silence, and then a small voice.

"Uh, I just wanted to say thanks for getting me out of the mud." It was the voice of that solid citizen and hometown jerk, Manuelito Alfonso Garcia.

Mogi, a little stunned, opened the door. Manny seemed a lot smaller now, a couple of feet below him.

Jennifer jumped to the door, smiled, and invited him in. Manny was a little hesitant, if not actually embarrassed, but he sat down as Mogi closed the door and rejoined the group.

"Uh, thanks for helping me out," he said. "It would have been a long walk to town." His bandanna was still in place, but his accent was less pronounced.

Mogi watched his sister. Jennifer could make a serial killer feel comfortable in an FBI interrogation room. She didn't make a big deal about the incident of the stuck car and talked to him like she talked to everyone else. Where she was getting the energy, he couldn't guess.

After a few minutes, Mogi's tiredness drained away, the teens relaxed, and the conversation got going. Even Rachel didn't seem to mind Manny's presence.

"Do you remember the professor's talk the other night?" Mogi asked.

"I didn't listen real close," Manny responded," but I liked the part about the old slave telling his son about some kind of bowl of blood. He's got a screw loose if he thinks any of the Indians around here ate people, though. They respect all life. They even say prayers over the animals they kill for food."

"Let me tell you some of the things we've been thinking about," Mogi said.

He described Chandler's ideas and showed the image in his phone of the riddle about the Womb of the Mother. He related the conversations with Mrs. Abeyta and her grandfather, bringing up his text with the lines about the legend, and then described the ideas about a hidden river in the lava flows, including seeing the whole area from the mesa. He didn't mention the professor being chased by the four men or the bashing of the pickup; he assumed that Manny knew about those things.

His train of thought was broken by a shuffling sound on the gravel outside. The others also heard it, but could see nothing when they looked out the windows. Rachel looked out the trailer door but saw nothing.

"Probably a raccoon. They're all over the place in the summer," Manny said.

Mogi went on with his analysis. "The biggest problem with looking for the Womb of the Mother is that it's connected to a river. But there's no river in El Malpais and there doesn't seem to ever have been. I think we're stuck."

"Yeah, don't look like any rivers out there to me. You really think that the magic whatever was real?" Manny asked. "You might be chasin' a ghost, man. And even if it was real, you expect to find it?"

Mogi was thinking that inviting him in may not have been such a good idea, but it was too late to bicker. "I read that if the Spanish were good at anything, it was record keeping. So, yeah, I think that the old slave's words were correct. If they were, then there is a spot someplace out in the lava beds that was called the Womb of the Mother. It had to do with a river, and there was some object that the Acoma people thought was magic, and it ended up being hidden in that same place."

"And, being as nothing has ever shown up," Jennifer said, "it could still be out there."

"And, if it's out there, it's worth searching for," Rachel chimed in, "if for no other reason than finding it would allow us to get that professor's butt out of the state and out of my dad's hair,"

Manny shook his head and gave a little grin. "Yeah, OK, so blowing that geek up is something I can probably get behind. My grandmother would love to see that happen. So, whatcha gonna do?"

"There's a photograph that's up on the wall at the monument headquarters," Mogi began, "and we think we've got a clue." He went on to describe the idea of a hidden river, and what the big cottonwoods on the south end of El Malpais might mean.

"We're going down there tomorrow," Jennifer broke in. "How about you go with us? We can always use another set of eyes."

The offer came as a surprise to Manny, who shifted in his seat. He wondered if he was really being asked to go along or was being made fun of, and then shrugged his shoulders. A small hint of embarrassment came into his face. "Uh, well, sure. I can help out."

"We'll leave at eight in the morning. You'll need a jacket, flashlight, water, and a daypack. I have an extra if you need one."

The young man's head was bobbing up and down. "Yeah, OK. I'll be here. I better go home and get ready. Goin' on an adventure!" he said with a grin.

After Manny left, Mogi locked the door and returned to the table.

Jennifer spoke first. "An even stranger end to a strange day. I'm going to go to bed before anything else happens."

Rachel laughed. "Me, too. I can't believe the jerk is going with us, but I'm more surprised that I'm looking forward to it a little. I'm just curious to see what happens. Who would have thought? You Franklins are something else."

Mogi laughed. "Well, the table we're sitting at turns into my bed, so you two take care of yourselves and I'll see you in the morning."

The two girls disappeared into the bedroom in the front of the trailer. Mogi started to fold the table away, but then didn't. So many things about the mystery had happened and yet hardly any firm facts had appeared. The violence—the professor's tires, his being chased, the pickup—had been a surprise. He didn't know Pueblo people would be that sensitive over a possible exposure of their past; it happened all the time with U.S. history. Nonetheless, he worried for Mr. Toffler and Rachel. This country was their home, and they had friends in all the different cultures. Would the violence touch them?

Mogi needed time to sit and think about things, especially if they were going into the lava beds the next day. He found a writing tablet and sat at the table. On an empty page, he carefully drew a line down the center of the first page. On the left side, he wrote what was known to have happened, like the old document that told the story. That the document existed was fact.

On the right side, he wrote what someone had described as happening, like the blood holder being put in the Womb of the Mother. The slave might have made that up. He read the original quote off his phone and wrote it down. He tried this for a while, trying to think of everything he could and placing it as either known or not known. He added the text of the riddle from Mr. Aguilar, some dates of the conquistadors, details of the Pueblo Revolt, and when Diego de Vargas came back.

The list was growing and Mogi wasn't able to put some things in one column or another, so he wrote them across the center line.

Dividing the information this way wasn't working. Mogi slumped against the seat back and ran his fingers through his hair. The frustration and discouragement were back. Everything seemed a long shot.

He stared at the piece of paper and realized how little he had.

Three hundred years. He was working to solve a mystery three hundred years old. What made him think he could waltz right in and solve it now?

Only a fool would think like that, a fool who always performed in front of his friends and family. Rachel must think he's a real bozo.

Mogi was tired all over, numb to feeling anything. Exhausted.

"Uh, oh. Things must be serious—he's making lists."

It was Jennifer. "The light was on, so I figured you were still up. You'd probably be better off going to sleep." She sat beside him and shuffled through the pages he had written.

Mogi smiled a little smile. "Yup—gotta make my lists. No good without my lists."

"So, any flashes of insight?" she asked.

"Not a glimmer."

"And you're feeling bad about it?"

"Well, yeah, I'm feeling stupid. Even if the original story is true—the one Chandler gave at the talk—it's been three hundred years. If anything could possibly be found, it would have been found."

"That's not true," she said. "There are lots of treasures yet to be found. However, I do think that it might take a miracle to do it in two days. You expect too much of yourself. Besides, it's not up to us to sort out the winners and losers in a local squabble over someone's statement about somebody eating somebody else. We're only visitors, right? Things like this take a long time to settle, if they ever settle at all."

"Wait a minute," Mogi said, leaning back against the cushion, "aren't you the one who's worrying about Rachel and her dad? This bad stuff affects them big time. And speaking of Manny, aren't you wishing you could do something to help him out?"

Jennifer took Mogi's pen and began doodling on his paper. "Yeah, well, OK. I wish I could do something. I hate it when people don't get along and I hate it worse when good people are caught up in messes like this. Rachel and her dad are really great, and Manny is just some kid who got lost in the shuffle of prejudice, parents, and social acceptance. I wish I could do something for all of them.

"What both of us have to remember is that we can only do what we can do. If an opportunity presents itself, we help. If not, well, we accept our limitations. The important thing is that we don't sacrifice ourselves for battles we can't win."

She got up with a yawn and a stretch. "You need to go to bed and let your brain work on your lists. I'll do likewise."

She ambled back to the bedroom, leaving Mogi with his elbows on the table, holding his head.

He lowered the table, spread out the cushions, and spread out a sheet and light blanket. It was only a minute or two after he crawled into bed that his body was asleep. But his mind was still sorting through the papers.

He dreamed he was at the pueblo, near the edge, looking down at the Cultural Center, raising his arms and feeling the air flowing around him, surrounding him and lifting him up, lifting him high above El Malpais and the lava fields, seeing North Pelon behind him. He loved flying, swooping around, gliding, zooming close to the lava and then zooming back up. It was all so mysterious—the different flows, the lava tubes, the valley surrounded by the tall mesas.

A million hiding places. Millions of objects could be hidden and he'd never see a single one. Too many cracks, too many boulders piled together, too many tubes that ran forever, and everything was dark. No light to see what was hidden even if he knew where to look. He kept on flying around and around and now all the lava was running up to the edge of big piles of sand, huge dunes, big like mountains, but it was all sand, sand everywhere. The river next to the dunes was running, clear water running out of the mountains right into the sand, disappearing. He couldn't see it anymore, so he flew closer and closer and closer. . .

He jerked awake to the loud screech of tires and gravel. A car door slammed, and a few seconds later there was a loud banging at the door.

"Hey, open up!" a voice shouted.

CHAPTER

10

"**R**achel!"
It was Bob Toffler.
Mogi opened the door as Jennifer and Rachel stumbled in from the bedroom.

"Rachel," Mr. Toffler said with relief, clambering into the trailer. Grasping his daughter by her shoulders, he said, "There's been some ugly business and I needed to make sure you were all right."

He gave her a squeeze, wincing slightly as he wrapped a heavily bandaged left arm around her. Mogi shoved the cushions aside, resurrected the table, and everyone sat down.

"Somebody took a bucket of blood and threw it on the door of Dr. Chandler's room at the motel. The police don't have a clue who did it, although I don't know how hard they're working at it. Then I got a call from the Information Center. Somebody broke the front door lock, went inside, and splashed a few more buckets of blood all over the floor and the books. They were gone before the rangers in the house trailer out back could get their clothes on."

"Please tell me it was animal blood," Jennifer said.

"We're sure it was, probably from a pig. They had several gallons."

"Did anything happen to the professor?" Mogi asked.

"I don't know—nobody can find him." There was a hint of worry in Mr. Toffler's voice. "The night attendant at the hotel called the police when the blood was discovered. Chandler's room was empty when the police got there, and his car was gone, too. If he was missing when the vandals got to him, maybe that's why they came after me."

He raised his bandaged arm and rested it on the table. Reaching into his pocket with his other hand, he pulled out a crumpled piece of paper and spread it on the table.

"This came through my bedroom window, tied to a rock. I jumped out of bed before I knew what was going on and slipped. I cut my arm a couple of times on the broken glass."

The writing was in big block letters, written with a black marker:

MORE BLOOD TO COME BUT
NEXT TIME IT WILL BE <u>YOURS</u>

"The police couldn't make much out of it. I'm not sure if it was for me personally or if it's just that I'm a public figure." He yawned. His voice had grown tired, and he stood up to go.

"You guys make sure you stick together and let me know where you are. Keep your cell phones on, but remember that you may be out of service range. I've got to get back to town and start sorting this mess out."

He excused himself and was soon driving away.

It was a little after six o'clock. There was no reason to go back to bed, so the teens busied themselves with straightening up the trailer. Mogi was quiet until he'd gotten the mess of his bed straightened out, washed the dishes from the night before, and made pancakes for breakfast. He looked up at the girls as they slid into their seats.

"We can't stop now," he said, looking at Jennifer and Rachel. "Maybe this is really dumb and we may find absolutely nothing, but we've got to try. If somebody doesn't do something, nothing will change, and people will be in a world of hurt."

"Agreed," the girls replied.

Manny pulled up at about eight o'clock. He had heard about the incidents with the blood, but had not heard about the rock thrown through Mr. Toffler's window. His neighborhood, which was mostly Hispanic, had been noisy with accusations the evening before. Somebody had sworn that he'd heard the professor had proof that human sacrifices had been performed at the pueblos, and that all of the sacrifices had been Spanish children.

"All sorts of stories are being made up. Nobody knows the truth, but nobody's looking for it either," Manny said. "Even my mom is mad because she knows it can't be true, and if she's mad, then the pueblos must be really getting whipped up. I didn't hear much about what's going to happen tonight, but it could be worse."

Nobody knew who had done the blood slinging. Maybe it was just a bunch of locals playing a nasty game, having fun watching the panic. It could be like the thrill of a Halloween prank for them.

That's a lot of blood just for thrills, Mogi thought.

After they loaded their daypacks into the back of the Blazer, Rachel headed toward town. Heading east on Interstate-40, they drove until the highway branched south to Highway 117. It took less than an hour to get to the south end of El Malpais where the lava flows ended.

The sky was overcast and a breeze rustled the stalks of grass along the road, but Mogi didn't see any dark curtains hanging from the bottom of the clouds. Absorbed in the landscape as Rachel drove, he noticed that yesterday's rain had changed everything. Moisture had given a luster to the dull browns and blacks of the rocks. All the vegetation, as with anywhere in the Southwest after a good rain, immediately looked greener and richer. Sunflowers along the edges of the flows and across the fields next to the road glowed in contrast to the asphalt.

"Once we're at the cottonwoods," Mogi said to the others, "we'll follow the slope of the lava beds because the ground underneath should be the same slope, which any water would have followed. We'll also try to find some place where water would have come close to the surface. It might be in a lava tube or a regular cave, or maybe just a deep crevice."

Passing the lava beds, Rachel turned onto a dirt road, headed west. "This road goes across the bottom of the monument, but it gets really squirrelly as it joins the roads on the other side," Rachel said. "That's why we drove around the long way. The road's pretty rough, so I'm going to slow down. Everybody watch and let me know if you see any tracks we should follow."

Twenty minutes later, several tall cottonwood trees appeared a few hundred yards to their right. They had seen no side roads, and none were indicated on the map, so, getting as close as they could, they pulled onto the grass, shouldered their packs, and started walking. About ten minutes after leaving the Blazer, they reached the oasis.

Huge cottonwood trees lined up in a southerly direction, their big limbs intermixed and drooping almost to the ground. The bark was almost white, the leaves a shiny green. A tall layer of grass curled up around the trunks.

"Wow," Jennifer said. "This is like a terrarium, one of those glass jars where they grow plants and stuff."

The four companions walked beneath the big limbs, their hiking boots whipping the long grass. The air was thick with the odor of vegetation and moisture.

"OK," Mogi said. "Even without a river that we can see, there's obviously water feeding these trees. Let's see what it looks like on top of the lava."

Walking north through the trees and bushes, they came to end of the heavy vegetation. Beyond was a tall, rounded bulge of lava, like a huge swell of black rock had run out of energy and just stopped. It was close to twenty feet tall.

They found their way up the bulge and, once on top, surveyed the country ahead of them. Using the monument map with the locations of the major volcanoes marked, Mogi took a pen and drew a curving line that, looking at the slope of lava coming toward them, was a guess at the direction of the lava coming from the closest volcano and going to the trees behind them.

"OK, so here's the idea. All this vegetation means that there's a source of water under the ground. If it's below the ground here, maybe there's some kind of spring or something that's above the ground up the valley, hidden by the lava. Drawing the line like this doesn't mean that the lava flow lines up with the direction of the water, but it should at least give us a direction to start with. The riddle also said something about a hill, so it should be in that direction, too."

Rachel and Jennifer moved to the left until fifty yards or so were between them and the boys. They all promised to stay in sight of each other.

The going was rough and a strain on the ankles as well as on their boots; it was much rougher than the lava tube tour. Being on the forward edge of what must have been waves of flaming lava pouring from a recent volcano, the cracks and crevices were larger and hiking them safely required more concentration. Every so often, they stopped to check their location and guess at their heading, but they didn't stop for long. A sense of urgency pushed them forward.

Had Mogi not been so focused, he would have noticed that they were not alone. Flitting from rock to bush to rock, a shadowy figure followed them at a distance, watching carefully, waiting patiently, as the teen-agers made their way up the lava.

Mogi felt a growing feeling of disappointment. What would indicate water inside the lava? Should they be putting their ears to the rock to listen for water flowing? Did the river show up only in a rainstorm? Where did the rainwater go? The slave's riddle mentioned a hill. There were lots of hills, as far as he was concerned. Was one special? Would it still look special after three hundred years?

He just didn't know. Maybe this would turn out to be yet another way he would embarrass himself. It had been his idea to work on the mystery, and his idea to search the lava beds. A three-hundred-year-old mystery and he actually thought he was going to find the mysterious object?

Yup, looking stupid was right around the corner.

The thing to do, he coached himself, is to stop every so often and examine everything around me, over and over again. Does anything look unusual? Pay attention to the plants because they might indicate water. Pay attention to direction of the lava. Pay attention. Look everywhere.

Manny did not say much. No longer shy about being with the others, he was as active as Mogi when it came to looking around. If he saw something unusual, he pointed it out. If he thought of some idea related to the mystery, he told Mogi about it. Being out on the land reminded him of the walks he used to take with his grandmother, far out into the valley floor around the Acoma mesa. He had liked every walk—there was something about the land that tugged at his heart and made him feel part of it.

Signaling each other, all four came together to take a break. They had been hiking almost an hour and a half.

The shadowy figure a hundred yards behind them stopped as well and slipped behind a boulder.

"When you were mapping the flows, do you remember any hills?" Mogi asked Rachel.

"I've thought about that," she replied. "I saw some places where lava flowed around a tall hill. The hill had to be, oh, twice as high as the thickness of the lava. Anyway, the lava piles up on one side, flows around the hill, and joins together on the other side, just like water flows around a rock. On the down slope of the hill is usually an area of exposed ground before the lava comes together again. I forget exactly where they were, though."

After the group had rested, they set out again. Mogi and Manny switched routes with the girls.

About fifteen minutes later, the boys heard a yell. Looking over, they could see Rachel pointing ahead of her.

Two hundred yards in front was what she had described— a barren hilltop a hundred or so feet higher than the surrounding land. The hill had stood its ground as lava pushed around it. The hill looked like a green-brown bump in a sea of black.

Mogi's heart pumped wildly as he and Manny joined the girls in racing to the base of the hill. It was the only unusual feature they had found, and it was a clear match to at least one part of the slave's riddle.

Stopping on the closest edge of lava, they found an open spot of ground just below the hill. It had filled with water from the rainstorms and was slowly soaking into the dirt, leaving a thick layer of mud along its outer edges.

Mogi walked on the lava around the open spot and climbed to the top of the hill, dodging the few juniper trees dotting its surface. Far in the distance from where they had come, Mogi could see the tops of the cottonwoods. That meant that it was at least possible that any water from where he was standing could make it to the oasis.

The others had circled around the hill and were working around the bottom, pushing through some of the larger bushes, searching intensely for any kind of opening, either in the hill or in the surrounding lava. As Jennifer jumped to a patch of dry ground, a rabbit shot across the mud and disappeared behind a bunch of sunflowers growing between the hill and the lava.

Mogi moved across the top of the hill, came down the incline, and stepped onto the lava next to Rachel.

"We didn't see an opening of any kind," Rachel said in a disappointed voice. "There's nothing here."

Mogi shook his head, remembering his discouragement of the night before. It seemed like the perfect place, matching the description of the professor's document, but there was no cave, no opening, no Womb of the Mother.

While on top, he had searched for other hills. He could see other bumps, but they were much farther up the valley and much farther from the cottonwood oasis. This hill seemed to be their best and maybe only shot at finding anything. He didn't want it to end without something, anything that might help Rachel and her dad.

Mogi closed his eyes. He remembered what he had seen that morning, what he had learned from the aerial photograph in the monument headquarters, and what he had noticed in his panorama. The cottonwoods, the lava, the map, the flow of the land, the hill, the sunflowers, the mud, the water, the bushes, the different flows, the textures, the road, the location of the tubes. He patiently worked through the images.

"Let me go back up," he said to Rachel as he opened his eyes. "Maybe I missed something."

Struggling up the steep hill again, he took his binoculars out of his pack and surveyed the land to the north. He scanned the flow up and down, wishing and hoping, but found nothing particularly unusual. He looked at his phone again and compared the pictures to where he now stood. Disappointed, he took giant steps down the side of the hill. Halfway, he slipped and slid with a shower of gravel and dirt. Regaining his balance, he moved to the front of the depression where the others sat on the edge of the lava.

"There're a couple of other hills, but they're much farther to the west," he said. "Other than those, I didn't see anything that wasn't covered with lava, and I didn't see any hill of lava that I would call much taller than anything around it."

Maybe the whole thing was wrong. Maybe the land of hard-walking meant some other place. Maybe they were miles off. Maybe they were centuries off.

Manny had watched Mogi come down the hill, watched him slip, and watched him walk toward them.

"That's weird," he said matter-of-factly.

"What?" Jennifer asked.

"A few minutes ago, you spooked a rabbit, and he ran over there under the sunflowers." Manny pointed to the tall stalks with the bright yellow blooms. "When Mogi came down, he knocked a bunch of gravel down onto the same spot, but the rabbit didn't run out." He turned to Jennifer. "If I'd been that rabbit, I would have found a new hiding place pretty quick."

Jennifer looked at him and at the rabbit's tracks in the mud. The tracks went to the bushes and didn't come back. She looked at the others.

As if by signal, all four of them stood up and made their way to the sunflowers. Mogi lowered himself from the lava onto the mud below the stalks and promptly sank halfway up his boots. Grimacing at the muck, he grabbed hold of the sunflower stalks and started pulling. Rachel came over the top, slipped down the little slope to the left of the bushes, and pulled with him.

"Ayiii!" she cried. "There's an opening! Oh, my gosh, I think I'm going to faint!"

A bolt of excitement hit them all. Mogi turned into a pulling machine. Ignoring the mud, he put all of his strength into reaching, grabbing, pulling, and throwing. His hands were soon slippery with the green slime of squeezed stalks. The sunflowers and a couple of yucca plants had been a long time in the soil and it took effort to get them out.

Finally, enough of the big plants were moved to expose a narrow opening between the hill and the lava. Beginning with not much more than a couple of feet in length, Jennifer and Manny shoved back the loose gravel, dirt, sand, and mud until they had doubled the size of the opening.

The more they moved, the more they could see that the opening was the beginning of a tunnel. Soon the opening was big enough to crawl through.

"Before we go in, let's get our helmets on," Mogi said hurriedly, forcing himself to hold back.

Rachel passed the helmets around, keeping the one with the light. Mogi wiped his crusted hands on his jeans and pulled a lantern plus two ropes from his pack, which he gave to Manny and Jennifer.

"Those are the ropes from my Blazer," Rachel said with surprise.

"And I brought my dad's lantern, too," Mogi replied with a grin, not trying to hide his pride in secreting the items away.

"We should leave some kind of marker outside, in case someone comes looking for us. It's a sure thing that they wouldn't be able to track us in this country," Manny said.

After five minutes, they had gathered up enough loose rocks to build a cairn about three feet high. Manny took off his bandanna and tied it around the top rock.

"I need to buy a new one, anyway. This one's getting kind of greasy," he said with a grin.

"OK," Mogi said to Rachel. "You have our flashlights?"

"What?" she said. "They were in the box in the back of the Blazer. I told you to get them."

"Uh, I thought you said you'd bring them," Mogi said.

"I always give the flashlights out before we start hiking. Are you telling me I didn't?" Rachel said incredulously. "Oh, shoot! And I left my phone there too!"

"I've got a flashlight," Manny said.

"OK, OK," Jennifer said. "Looks like Mogi and I forgot to get ours. But we've got our phones and they have a flashlight app on them. That's two phones, Manny's flashlight, Rachel's helmet light, and a lantern. That should be more than enough. We'll be okay."

"OK," Mogi said. "But the person in front, which is me, I guess, since I got all of you into this, should carry Manny's flashlight so we can see in front of us. We'll leave the phones off until we need them, and we'll put Rachel in the back with her helmet light. That should give us enough light to see where to put our feet."

Mogi was thin, but the slit was still a tight fit, and it took a while for him to learn how to keep from scraping his legs on the hard sides of the tunnel. Thankfully, the hole grew larger and the floor of the hole became mostly sand.

"Very interesting," Mogi said to the others as he moved through the opening. "The lava is on my right, the ground is on my left. The ground is looking like sandstone, so maybe it's a cliff or something, or maybe even an overhang. That's probably why the lava didn't flow up next to it."

He entered a taller part of the passageway and rose up on his knees. "From what I see in front of me, the passage stops," Mogi said, and then moved closer. "Oh, wait. It's a drop-off. The passage drops into a vertical shaft."

Everyone squeezed next to him to see what he had described.

"What now?" Jennifer asked.

"We need to see what we're looking at," Mogi said, removing his pack. He took out the lantern, put his pack back on, and then tied Jennifer's rope to the lantern's handle. He flipped the switch on the battery-powered lantern, giving an immediate burst of light, and lowered it over the edge.

Four pairs of eyes hunched over the edge to watch.

It was a circular shaft, not more than fifteen feet deep. At the bottom, a path led off in another direction. Now visible in the light, they could see that crude steps had been cut into the side of the shaft.

"You missed something," Rachel whispered, pointing off to the side.

Mogi pulled the lantern up. A couple of feet from the hole, back against the lava, several short logs had been jammed into a crack. The tattered remnants of an old rope hung from the center of the logs.

"That is definite proof that this was a place where people came," Rachel said. "The steps in the shaft were carved out to hold their feet, while they held onto that rope. I don't see why we can't do the same thing with a rope of our own."

Below the logs was a slightly terrified rabbit, which immediately dashed through their legs and scurried out the opening behind them.

With Manny's rope tied around the logs and tested with Mogi's weight, the teens nervously descended the steps in the sides of the shaft. They gathered at the bottom and started forward on the new path.

"Wait," Manny asked. "What about the rope?"

The others hadn't thought about it.

"We'll need it on the way back, so I guess we have to leave it," Mogi answered. He didn't know what else to do. He hoped the other rope would be enough for whatever lay ahead.

The companions now walked upright, though the path was narrow, sometimes forcing them to barely squeeze past the walls on both sides. The path had also steepened and turned from packed dirt into a sand and gravel floor. Every now and then, Mogi stopped the group, turned completely around with the lantern held above him, and thought about whatever he saw.

He reached out and felt the sides. It was the same kind of smooth sandstone as the bluffs they had passed on Highway 117.

"You know what this reminds me of?" he asked as he turned to the group. "Back in Utah and in northern Arizona, we have what are called 'slot canyons.' They're really narrow canyons, almost crevices, carved out of the sandstone by streams running over the rock for hundreds of years. This makes the canyons narrow and deep and the walls very smooth and curvy. That's what I think this is. If so, the passage should get wider at the bottom."

"Mogi!" Jennifer cried. "What do you smell?"

Mogi had been too absorbed in thinking to notice. He took a deep breath and smiled broadly.

Water.

CHAPTER

They snaked through the narrow passageway, the scent of water growing stronger, combined with the smells of sand and rock. Around the edges of the light from the lantern, the flitting shadows gave the narrow way an unreal appearance, like a picture moving from 3D to 2D and back.

Mogi's heart was beating hard with a combination of excitement, desperation, and raw fear. He was sure they had found the Womb of the Mother; it was too incredible to think that the text from the letter and the riddle of the slave had led them to anything else. But the proof—the proof!—must be ahead of them.

The slope of the passageway increased and Mogi slowed to be more careful. As he held the lantern in front of him, the narrow slot ended, and they now passed into a larger canyon, much wider than where they had come. The sides of the canyon disappeared into the darkness above them.

A small stream of crystal clear water flowed through the middle of the opening's floor, a flat floor of sand and gravel between the canyon's rock walls.

"Woohoo!" Mogi cried. "It's a river! We found it!"

They whooped and hollered, the sounds muffled as they spread inside the chamber. Mogi leaned down, ran his hand through the water, and then held the lantern high to reflect against the surrounding walls.

It had taken twenty or more minutes to reach the end of their narrow confines. Mogi knew exactly what they had found. It *was* a slot canyon, carved out of the sandstone of the valley, and it had to have been here before the lava ever flowed.

"The lava must have been so thick and the canyon so narrow that it flowed right over the top without falling in," he said. "The stream must be fed by a spring—it's been flowing all these years."

Finally quieting from their discovery, they stopped to pull their jackets from their packs.

"I'm leaving my pack here," Jennifer said as she propped it against the crack in the wall, "so we know which passageway is the way out."

With the pack in place, they moved downstream.

"Man, I've never been in a place like this," Manny said. "Standing on the cliffs at Sky City is pretty cool, making like a bird and everything, but this is totally something else. It's like being back inside your mama."

"Little brother," Jennifer said as Mogi examined every nook and cranny of the walls along the stream, "we need to remember that we can't stay too long. The lantern won't last forever."

"You're right," Mogi said. "We need to get down to business. There's no doubt in my mind that this is the Womb of the Mother, which means we ought to be seeing something related to the pueblo. I've looked as we walked and haven't seen any signs of humans at all. We've only come one direction, though, so maybe it's the other way. Any ideas on how to search this place?"

Mogi wished they had more time. He wanted to examine every square inch. If there were ever a special place, this was it.

"How about splitting up?" Manny proposed. "Two go downstream and two go upstream."

"That's a little scary for me," Jennifer said quickly. "I've seen a lot of films where everybody gets separated and the monster eats them one by one. Maybe we could just go twice as fast in each direction?"

Rachel was more comfortable with tight, dark places. She offered to go upstream and check it out, but no one thought her going alone was a good idea. After all, Mr. Toffler had told them to stick together. They finally decided to go with Manny's idea.

Mogi lined out the situation: "Rachel, with her headlamp, and Manny, with his flashlight, will go up the canyon. Only use one light if you can. Jennifer and I, with our two cell-phones and the lantern, will go down the canyon, but we won't use the lantern until we have to.

"Let's give ourselves twenty minutes. We need to be quick about it. Go as fast as you can and call out if you find something. If you haven't found something in twenty minutes, turn around and come back to this entrance. This canyon could run for miles, so we might have to come back prepared to spend a day.

"Keep your eyes out for anything unusual. We've got to clear up this mystery before somebody pulls another bloodbath prank."

Mogi and Jennifer watched the bouncing lights of Rachel and Manny as they turned and moved upstream. Mogi turned on the flashlight app of his phone, held it directly ahead of him, and then turned off the lantern. It gave off much less light than the lantern, making the space around them dark and gloomy. He gave the lantern to Jennifer.

Setting a good pace down the middle of the stream, Mogi and Jennifer watched for any signs of humans. They saw nothing. The walls and floor appeared untouched, and there was not a blade or stem of any vegetation on the sandy floor.

The walls of the canyon widened as they went, but the ceiling height decreased dramatically. Mogi could now see that everything above them was the black rock of lava. Further on, they found chunks of lava on the floor.

"We must be getting to the end, where the lava flow would have fallen into the canyon because it was too wide to flow across," Mogi said, "and we've got another two minutes before we need to turn around." As he spoke, he noticed that his phone's battery life had dropped by half.

"Shoot!" he said. "I forgot to plug my phone in last night. Oh, man!"

They should probably turn back now, he thought, as he moved around a pile of lava boulders, but he was desperate to find the end of the canyon.

One more minute and the stream disappeared. It spread out into a flat area of sand, pooled a little bit behind a rise in the floor, and then was gone. "After a few hundred years, that's probably a very deep pool of quicksand," he said.

Shining his light ahead, Mogi saw that a wall of lava plunged into the floor directly in front of them.

Jennifer was growing anxious. She hadn't turned on her phone yet, but she knew the battery was not going to last as long as she wanted. Making the phone a flashlight used up the charge like crazy.

"Let's go!" she called as her legs began to shake. "I'm getting scared, and I think these walls are closing in on us!"

Mogi caught up with her and moved ahead. Despite the coolness of the air, he began to sweat.

I hope coming down here wasn't a big mistake, he thought. He was remembering the total darkness of the lava tube—they would be in big trouble if the lights quit working. Maybe they should have gone back to the Blazer for the flashlights.

The two moved quickly, as fast as they could, splashing water across the sand and gravel as they sloshed up the stream. Mogi wondered how Rachel and Manny were doing.

Then he heard the screams.

*   *   *

After leaving the Franklins, Rachel and Manny had moved quickly upstream. They recognized the narrow entrance as they passed.

"Look!" Rachel pointed to a sandy spot twenty feet past the entrance. Pieces of wood lay in piles. The two of them moved over to inspect the area. The ends of the wood had been chopped.

They moved on.

Rachel was studying the canyon wall as she walked and, distracted, tripped on a stone in the stream. She fell forward, her helmet flying off into the water.

Her light went out.

She got up and slapped the light a couple of times in disgust, but it remained dark. "I must have broken the bulb, or else the connections didn't like the water. Shoot!"

Manny took the lead with his flashlight, and they tried to quicken their pace.

Manny had brought the flashlight because Mogi asked him to, but he never really expected to use it. He had no idea how old the batteries were. He pointed the beam in the direction they were going, moving the light from side to side.

Rachel kept her hand on Manny's back as they walked, which slowed them down. She began to move from side to side behind him, hoping to see more. The cave narrowed and she ran her hand along the walls to keep her balance.

The wall of the cavern widened suddenly, and her hand, reaching for the wall, missed having the sandstone to touch. Overextending her reach, she stumbled to the left, away from the light, and went to her knees.

In the dimness, in the quickness of the fall, all she saw was a grinning skull coming toward her.

CHAPTER

12

Hearing was difficult because sounds bounced off the narrow walls, but there was no need to make out words—a series of screams came rocketing down the canyon in front of them.

Jennifer turned her phone's flashlight on, and the two ran as fast as they could.

They recognized the entrance as they ran past Jennifer's daypack. A hundred feet further, they found Rachel and Manny. Mogi turned the lantern on.

Rachel was trembling, and Manny's eyes were wide with terror. They sat on the right bank of the stream, holding each other, staring straight ahead.

"Rachel! What happened?" Jennifer shouted, leaning down and shaking Rachel to get her attention. Rachel looked up at her and pointed a silent finger across the stream.

In the light of the lantern, a wide sand beach lay under an outward curve in the smooth sandstone wall. On the beach lay a full skeleton of a man, bones glistening white against the brown sand, his eyeless sockets staring.

Jennifer gave a short scream and jumped back. A wave of quivering shook Mogi's body, but he stayed rooted in the middle of the stream, frozen. The other three scooted closer to the wall.

A few seconds passed before Mogi swallowed and began to breathe again. He moved toward the skeleton, and Manny crossed the stream to join him.

The skeleton was stretched spread-eagle on the stream bank, each arm reaching above the head and away from the body, the legs likewise. Each wrist and ankle had been strapped to wooden stakes driven into the sand, but the straps had long rotted away. Mogi focused on each piece of wood. The skeleton was double-staked—each limb tied to one stake, then the strap pulled and tied onto another stake. If the victim managed to pull out the first stake, it would have done no good. The second, farther away than the first, would have kept the tension on the strap.

There were a few tatters of cloth under what seemed to be a leather tunic, the remains of a broad leather belt, a sheathed dagger still dangling from a thong, and other scatterings of material. But the most conspicuous feature was the chainmail shirt draped over the ribcage.

"He must have been a Spanish conquistador," Mogi said.

Neither the document nor the legends had said anything about a conquistador. How would a Spanish soldier have known about this place? The Womb of the Mother was hidden, sacred, and no place for the Spanish. The pueblo would never have allowed it.

Mogi looked closely at the straps. The hand and foot bones were broken and contorted, probably the result of the captive man straining against rawhide cords.

He had been alive when someone staked him down.

The girls stood and moved to the middle of the stream.

"I know you guys are really interested in this, but we've got to get out of here," Rachel said in an urgent voice. "We can't be left down here without lights."

Mogi pulled himself away from the man's deathbed and sloshed farther up the hidden canyon. Being on the move again calmed the troop a bit, and their breathing slowed. Whatever they had imagined in this adventure, a skeleton had not been included.

The streambed meandered while the walls narrowed again for about ten feet and then curved around a corner. As the four moved with the stream, the light lit up a large room ahead of them. The chamber was bulb-shaped at the bottom, narrowing again above them. The stream ran directly through the center, with a sandy beach on the right. The light caught several objects on the beach and the far wall.

All four of them stood in wonder, stunned by what they saw. Pots.

Clay pots of all sizes and shapes. Pots crowded on the sand, next to the wall, on shelves carved out of the canyon wall. Pots decorated with designs.

Blankets lay across the sand and up the wall. There were woodcarvings and decorative shields with feathers. Large spears leaned across the curving sandstone.

No one said anything. The scene unfolded before them as if curtains were pulled back on a stage. It was almost too much to take in. The teens shuffled forward, stepping out of the water onto the beach, avoiding touching the blankets at their feet.

Not all the sloshing sounds ceased after they were out of the water, but they did not notice.

Manny's flashlight, which he had forgotten to turn off, burned bright and then went dark. He tried pounding it against his hand, but nothing produced as much as a tiny glow.

A large blanket of intricately woven patterns of reds, blues, and yellows covered the sand in the center of the display. Around it were pots of every size, painted mostly black on white. To the right, a large drum with a tanned skin cover sat next to the wall, a large shield of leather and feathers hanging above it. Other objects like it were propped on the other side. Their eyes soon rested on the center of the display. In a shelf carved out of the wall, sat a small wooden box.

Setting the lantern on the blanket, Mogi carefully stepped over the objects on the floor to see the box up close. It was a simple box, with the sides made of planed wood, the corners fitted together with interlaced joints, and a top with small clasps and hinges of hammered metal.

It was a box not made by the ancient Acoma people.

He reached for the box, gently lifted it, stepped back into the center of the blanket, knelt, and placed it on the floor. The others moved around him. There were two iron clasps, which he undid. Carefully prying the lid fully back, he could hear the others holding their breath. Reaching in, he circled his hands around a bundle of stiff leather wrapping. He lifted the bundle, feeling a single object inside. He undid the folds and carefully pulled back the covering.

The lantern suddenly dimmed and then went out.

CHAPTER

Late October, 1692
(the day before the Spaniards' return)

The governor of the Acoma people crawled into the entrance to the Womb of the Mother. Holding a burning torch, he crawled carefully between the ground and the hard rock. When he reached the ledge, he tossed down his spare torches, hung his legs over the side, grabbed the rope fixed above him, and swung out over the shaft.

The torch, held between his teeth, guided him down the shaft as he stepped gently to the floor below. Inhaling deeply, the aroma of the water filled his head and swelled his spirit.

A sacred place. Holy.

He moved through the passageway to the river and then walked upstream to the large chamber that held his people's offerings. He stuck the end of the torch in the sand and lit another. When the altar was fully lighted, he removed a bundle of clothing from his sling. After unwrapping and carefully laying the white buckskins on the blanket, he removed his clothes.

Naked, he washed in the stream, singing songs of cleansing and praise. He was in the Womb of the Mother, surrounded by holiness. Before any rituals were done, he must be clean.

He dried himself with sand, brushed the grains off, and put on the ceremonial buckskins, carefully tying each knot, straightening the beads, and smoothing the leather to hang straight. He took the wooden box out of the sling and walked on the blanket before the altar. He moved a large clay pot from the center hollow in the wall and replaced it with the box. It was now safe. His purpose was fulfilled.

The governor knelt at the foot of the shrine, his eyes closed, and sang the songs of his ancestors. His reverence was right, his holiness good. All was correct; all had been done well.

The torches were burning low as he finished. He changed his clothes, repacked the garments, lit the third torch, extinguished the other two, laid them next to the chamber's entrance, and followed the stream down.

It is complete, thought the governor. The blood holder is safe.

He moved up the rocky slope, climbed up the steep well, crawled out the opening, and returned to his people.

*   *   *

A day later, a terrified man hurriedly slid between the hard rocks and the soft stone. He almost fell over the edge of the steep part, grabbing at the rope at the last second and clumsily lowering himself. He'd had enough time to fashion only one torch, patching it together as he scrambled his way across the lava.

The Spanish soldier had almost caught him, but he had sprinted among the black boulders at the edge of the flow, beyond where the Animal of War could go. The soldier was slow to dismount and prepare his weapons, giving the fleeing man time enough to get ahead.

Hurrying down the narrow passageway, the man found himself at the stream, confused by which way to go. Finally, seeing the marks in the sand beside the stream, he followed them, moving as fast as he could, the flames from his torch lashing against the walls of rock, until he stumbled into the round-shaped chamber.

It took him several seconds to take in the appearance of the chamber and the altar. Inner voices warned him of violating the holiness of the place, but he could no longer keep himself from the panic in his throat and mind.

He found the mostly-used torches on the floor and lit them from his own. With the added light, he recognized the box that had been set into the sandstone wall. He had seen it only twice over the years but knew it immediately.

As he grabbed the box, he heard the noise of gravel falling and an angry voice echoing up the path.

The soldier had followed him!

The man, sweat pouring from his forehead, panicked as thoughts screamed inside his head. He tore at the clasps and dumped the contents onto the blanket.

I will wait for the Spaniard, he swore in his mind, and he will see my gift for him. He will take the gift and let me go! He will let me go!

Downstream, the soldier was irritated. He hated the darkness and the narrowness and the rock and the cave and the stench of smoke in the air and the slippery tunnel, and he especially hated the squirmy insect of a man he was hunting. He had left his horse and armor where the black rocks began and followed the man at a relentless pace, making huge strides with his long legs. His leather boots were scarred and ripped, but he was obsessed with capturing his prey and would not turn back.

He lit the candle he always carried in his tunic, and it provided enough light as he slipped and fell his way down the passageway. Now he focused on the yellow glow of light in the tunnel ahead of him. He was anxious to find this worm and send him to his death.

The Spaniard splashed through the stream into the large chamber to find the Acoma insect kneeling before him, holding some silver trinket up to him. With a mighty swing of his hand, the soldier knocked the trinket to the side and gave a full kick of his boot to the pathetic face, shoving him into the waters of the stream.

Reeling from the blow, blood running from his lips and nose, the small man was confused. The Spaniard had disregarded the object of his own god! The holy thing had been slammed aside, treated as nothing. He couldn't understand it.

A thought pounded its way through the pain. The leaders had been wrong! They had all been wrong! The blood holder meant nothing. There was no power!

The large soldier bore down on him. The big leather boots, however—soaked thoroughly—failed to find a good hold on the fine-grained sand and gravel of the stream bottom. As the big man rushed forward, his feet slid from beneath him and he crashed into the stream, sending sprays of water across the chamber. The smaller, quicker man grabbed the burning torch and shoved it into the larger man's face.

Screaming with pain, the soldier plunged his face into the water and pulled up just in time to see the smaller man perched above him and the pot coming down upon his head.

Once, twice, three times the pot hit him until it shattered into a hundred shards.

The smaller man labored to drag the unconscious soldier through the water, but he had known a lifetime of hard work. He found stakes, rawhide, and a mallet left in a storage place for the upkeep of the shrine and used them to strap the man fast to the ground.

Once he finished, he found the blood holder among the wreckage of the fight, carefully wrapped it again with deerskin, placed it in its box, and returned it to the center shelf. He gathered up the shards of the broken pot, smoothed the sand, and straightened the blankets, returning the shrine to its original condition. He hoped that the honor he showed would work, in some way, to bring mercy to his people. Perhaps the magic would now work because a soldier had been sacrificed.

He left the torch to burn itself out, giving his enemy a dim light by which to see his death coming, a little more time before the darkness robbed him of his mind.

He took the Spaniard's boots—objects he had always admired—and returned up the narrow passage to the entrance. He wiped the tracks from the dirt and laid brush against the entrance. The boots were too big, requiring him to use all of the wrappings on his feet to keep them from falling off, but they were better than his sandals.

Retracing his steps across the land of hard-walking, the Acoma man found the horse tied to a tree. A conquistador's helmet and breastplate hung from the saddle, and other armor pieces were stacked on the ground. The boots had worked for the hard rocks, but they were much too clumsy for regular land; he threw them down a large crack in the rock, along with the armor.

The man to whom they belonged was now screaming in terror in the smoky darkness far beneath the black rock.

The Acoma man made several attempts at riding the horse before deciding that running with his own legs would have to do.

The Spanish army, having negotiated the allegiance of Acoma Pueblo with surprisingly little resistance, were on their way to Zuni Pueblo to continue reestablishing their rule. When the column of men and horses came upon the lone

Acoma native, staggering on the edge of exhaustion and making some incomprehensible plea for mercy, they locked chains around his neck and set him to pace with the others.

They needed slaves in Mexico, and here was one more. Little did they know that they should have listened to what the small man was telling them.

Only in his dreams did the new slave of the Spanish empire ever return to the Womb of the Mother.

CHAPTER

14

Present Day

I t wasn't just dark in the Womb of the Mother. It was really, completely, no-light-whatsoever, horribly, terribly, frighteningly dark.

When Mogi had turned on the lantern, Jennifer had turned her phone off and put it back in her pocket. She now panicked, fumbling as she pulled it out, and the phone dropped onto the sand beneath her. She was immediately on her knees, running her hands desperately over the area where it might have fallen.

Feeling the smooth case, she opened it, flashed through the apps, and turned on the light.

She could hear the change in their breathing rates.

"Thank God," Rachel said. "Thank God."

It was helpful, but it did not fool anyone. They only had one cellphone for light and there was no guessing how long the charge would last. They needed to get out, now.

Mogi stuck the useless lantern sideways into his pack, replaced his newly found object in its box, and slid the box on top of the lantern. It stuck out, preventing the zipper from closing, but he wasn't about to spend more time on it. It was good enough.

He didn't have time to think about the item in the box, about how it solved the puzzle, or about how it explained everything.

Barely able to miss crashing into the sides of the narrow canyon, Mogi, Rachel, and Manny hurried down the stream behind Jennifer as she held the phone in front of her.

After going only a few dozen yards, Mogi suddenly felt hands grip his shoulders. Then he was spun around and pushed into the others. Bumping, stumbling, tripping, slipping, the friends fell over each other as the erratic movement of the light jerked across the walls and ceiling.

"I'll take that!"

The voice came out of the shadows as the wooden box was yanked from Mogi's pack.

"No!" Mogi yelled.

In an instant, the cellphone was ripped from Jennifer's hand and bashed against the canyon wall. The light went out instantly and forever.

A confusion of motion suddenly erupted. The teens called out, grasped for each other, stumbled in the water, and bumped into each other in a frenzy laced with panic and fear. Along with the others, Mogi heard himself screaming.

Still struggling to right himself in the darkness, Mogi saw a flashlight turn on ahead and heard water splashing as a man dashed down the stream. The beam caught a face in the movement.

The professor!

Mogi managed to find a wall to lean against and pulled the others together. Trembling, they reached their hands out to find anyone to touch, anyone to hold.

The darkness provoked a crushing fear, with breaths coming fast, cries and whimpering automatic and unstoppable, and an involuntary turning and twisting of the body, fearing at any second that someone or something was grabbing at them.

"You guys!" Mogi said as he regained control of his voice. "Listen to me!"

"Let's pull it together," Rachel added.

Slowly, the ruckus quieted down, though their hands still held tight to whomever they touched.

"We don't need a light. We came in one way, we can get out one way," Mogi said, not so much out of confidence as from anger. And he was *angry*. He understood in a flash what had happened.

"The professor followed us. After what we said to him last night at park headquarters, he figured we had found some new clues."

Mogi then remembered the sound outside the trailer. It must have been the professor listening to their conversation. Mogi's cheeks grew hot and red and he could feel the rage in his hands.

"OK, give me your hands. Jennifer, you need to let me stand in the water."

She understood and did as he said. She knew that her brother had a remarkable gift of memory. It wasn't photographic, but it was enough that he could recall an incredible amount of detail from scenes that he had only glanced at.

"You can get us out of here?" she asked Mogi.

"You bet," he said, though his voice cracked with emotion. "I got you into this, and I will get you out."

The others held on to each other as Mogi pushed them into a line against the wall. That would keep them steady.

Taking a deep breath, he made his way to the stream and determined which direction it was flowing. He stood, faced downstream, closed his eyes, and took a deep breath.

The others heard him: one, two, three long deep breaths, and then silence.

Mogi remembered.

He remembered the slit above, then the entrance to the shaft, down the shaft to the canyon, running his hand against each side as he held the lantern in the other, feeling the smoothness of the sandstone.

Turning left, he remembered returning from the lower part of the canyon and turning on the lantern, its light opening up the darkness ahead of him and Jennifer as they ran. Curving this way, moving that way, seeing the conquistador as his bones lay tied to the stakes.

A few steps later and he was in the chamber. From left to right, he saw the pots, the rugs, the drums, the shields, the altar. He remembered Jennifer's light and the way she moved, how he and the others had followed her, and then a last glimpse as the professor ran from them, holding the stolen box in his arms.

Simple, really. Now all he had to do was play the scenes backwards.

"Everybody get behind me. Manny, you be in the rear behind Rachel, Jennifer's behind me. Feel the direction of the water against your feet? That's the direction we want to go. When you're ready, put your left hand on the shoulder in front of you and your other hand against the wall on the right."

The teens sorted themselves out and were soon lined up

"Everybody take a deep breath," Mogi said. "OK. We're going home."

He could feel the relief behind him; he knew his self-assurance was a comfort to the others. But in fact, he was terrified. He usually didn't mind the darkness, but that was typically a darkness that had a moon and stars in it. This absolute darkness frightened him to the bone.

The teens moved in a baby-step shuffle, finding that it took a certain cadence to not step on the feet in front of them. It was clumsy and slow, but Mogi's confidence grew. The critical thing was to not miss the entrance slot to the right. He assumed the professor had seen Jennifer's daypack and grabbed it, fully intending to slow his pursuers down.

He was worried that they had gone too far when his hand against the wall suddenly touched nothing. Bringing everybody to a halt, he ran his hands along the sides of the entrance, making sure it was the opening they needed.

It was.

The line of slow-moving bodies turned like a caterpillar and moved up the smaller canyon, with all hoping they would soon see the light at the entrance.

They held on to each other as best as they could, but often had to use both hands to keep their distance from the sides. The trail seemed steeper than they remembered, with more ledges, crevices, steps, and rocks, while the crevice felt narrower than they remembered, with more curves, edges, and turns.

In spite of telling himself over and over to keep his cool, Mogi couldn't help but imagine monsters and ghosts and dead bodies and live bodies and the professor grabbing his hand every time he reached into the darkness before him.

Breathe. Focus.

A crashing sound and a cry echoed down the passageway in front of them, muffled as it bounced past. As if by a hidden sense, each of them squatted on the floor and held their breath.

No other sounds came.

"What was that?" Jennifer asked in a low whisper, afraid that someone was now rushing toward them.

"I don't know," Mogi whispered back. He felt her hand give him a reassuring squeeze and he stood and shuffled forward. He had to force himself. A sound meant something was in the passageway with them, close to them, perhaps even right around the next curve or the next bump in the path.

Or maybe just an inch away.

Mogi felt the blood rush into his face and he began to tremble. Then Jennifer circled her arms around him.

"You can do this," she said. "You are an incredible person, and I am your sister. Where you go, I go. I will not leave you."

Breathe. Focus. He moved forward.

An eternity of twenty long minutes crept by. His eyes hurt from being held wide open and his nerves were exhausted from fitfully reaching into the emptiness ahead of him. But it was the ever-present feeling of terror, of having to move with no visual reference, of the clumsiness of his feet against a surface he could not see that kept him on the verge of panic.

Faintly, oh so faintly, he detected a glow ahead of him. His heart jumped. Afraid that it was only flashes from inside his eyelids as he blinked, he moved his head. The light didn't move with him.

They had to be close to the entrance. He lengthened his stride as the pale glow grew and moved over his head. Looking up, anxiously hoping they were in the vertical shaft, Mogi caught his foot on something and sprawled to the ground.

Right on top of a body!

He would have jumped three feet in the air if he had been standing. As it was, he screamed and leapt to his feet as fast as he could, his heart in his throat, his lungs gasping in panic.

Stumbling against Mogi as he fell, Jennifer screamed as she also stumbled over the body. She scrambled up frantically, caught in a tangle of legs, bumping first Mogi and then Rachel, against the sandstone wall.

The glow from above allowed Mogi's eyes to barely make out the body below him. He slowly knelt and started feeling around the faint outline. It wasn't hard to discover the lapels of a crumbled suit coat.

Professor Chandler was on the ground, unconscious.

Mogi looked up. The glow above revealed a pale ceiling of rock.

"We're at the shaft where we used the rope."

"The flashlight! Can you find his flashlight?" Rachel said.

Forcing themselves to feel the body and the ground around him, they searched for anything hard.

"Here!" Jennifer cried. She felt the outline of a flashlight and flicked the switch.

Oh, the blessing of light in darkness!

They immediately felt a rush of relief. After the initial elation, Mogi looked the professor over as Jennifer held the light. He lay in a crumpled position, a pile of Rachel's rope draped over him.

"Look." Mogi pointed at the end of the rope that they had left tied above, now on the ground. It was still wrapped around the length of an ancient tree limb. "The stick pulled out when he was climbing up. Serves the sucker right!"

"Maybe it was the spirits of the Indians," Manny said. "Maybe they've been waiting three hundred years for some kind of justice to bring the blood holder back. They've been waiting for us, and they've been waiting for him. And they want *us* to bring it home."

He spoke with a surprisingly calm voice, as if he had reached some kind of understanding. The others fell silent. Maybe it *was* the spirits.

"Let's get out of here," Mogi said. The others jolted into action.

Mogi found the wooden box in the professor's bag and slid it back into his own pack. He untied the rope from the log and wrapped it around his waist. Manny was charged with watching the professor for any movement.

"Hit him with the log if he moves," Rachel said.

"Jennifer, shine the light on the footholds in the wall," Mogi said. Without waiting for any questions or discussion, Mogi went up. With his long arms and legs, he climbed up the wall with spider-like movements, moving one foot, reaching the other side of the shaft with his arm, and then moving his next foot.

He reached the top quickly, sat on the edge of the well, and held the rope as the others climbed. After what they had been through, they could probably have ignored the rope and jumped the fifteen feet out of the hole.

Mogi pulled the rope up and left it at the top of the shaft. Jennifer did not return the flashlight to its owner.

They scrambled out of the slit and into the sunlight, grimacing and covering their eyes. It was a dim afternoon light on an overcast day, but it seemed bright as headlights. The two girls were almost giddy and practically sprinted across the lava for the Blazer. Mogi and Manny followed close behind.

"Oops," Manny cried out, jogging back to the hill. He retrieved the bandana from the pile of rocks and wrapped it around his head. "Can't leave my personality!"

The four teen-agers ran, skipped, jumped, dashed and jogged back to the vehicle. They had something that people needed to see.

When they reached the edge of the lava flow where they'd started, Mogi saw a couple of vehicles parked next to the Blazer and people walking into the cottonwoods. He recognized the family pickup parked next to the white park Suburban.

"Mom! Dad!" he screamed as he and his companions bounded down the slope of the lava's edge.

Hearing of the violence in Grants, Mogi's parents had returned to the trailer in mid-afternoon, worried when their children did not answer their cellphones. Following a note left by Jennifer describing their route, they immediately set out to find them and asked Bob Toffler to join them. Together, the parents had found the Blazer and were preparing to hike across the hard-rock country when they spotted the teen-agers moving along the edge.

All together under the sheltering leaves of the cottonwoods, everyone spoke at once. It took a long time to explain the events of the day and the night before.

Finally Mogi pulled the wooden box from his backpack and laid it on the tailgate of the pickup. The others gathered around him. As they looked at the contents of the box, what had happened three hundred years before became clear.

It was all about eating flesh and drinking blood.

CHAPTER

15

Mogi looked back from the front row of the auditorium. The lecture hall was standing room only.

The call for a meeting had gone out late in the afternoon. All of the town's officials, several police officers, pueblo officials, the local clubs—anyone of influence in the community—had been notified and asked to attend.

The atmosphere was tense. The violence of the night before had shocked people, filling them with fear that terrorists were on the loose. Rumors spread throughout the day—more blood, people carrying guns, who was going after whom, whose blood was going to spill next. The talk had resulted in fights in a couple of bars; gang members had thrown rocks at cars in one of the neighborhoods; a pig had been slaughtered and dragged behind a pickup.

People wanted to be angry, wanted to lash out at whomever was lashing out at them, feeling injustice—and wanting justice. With the announcement of the town meeting, many hoped the enemies had been identified, that maybe the bad ones had been caught.

A noisy audience greeted a lone man as he approached the microphone.

Bob Toffler was tired. He wasn't nervous, exactly, but afraid that the audience would not be willing to listen—not to him, not to anyone. He understood the need for just the right words.

"If I can have your attention, please," he said as the microphone squawked. It took almost a minute for the audience to settle down.

He looked out at the assembled people: Puebloans, Anglos, Hispanics, and mixed; individuals, couples, and groups. It was sobering to realize the issues each had brought along, and how fervently they all believed in their own perspective.

Mr. Toffler waited a few seconds more. His own silence slowly made the people more attentive. He decided that the direct method would work best.

He spoke with a loud voice, and a hint of a smile.

"OK, then, who called this meeting?"

The question took the crowd by surprise. Most assumed that he had called the meeting, or that he knew who had, or. . .what was going on?

After a few moments of confused murmuring, a man in the first row stood up. He moved quietly and deliberately to the microphone. A dead silence fell across the room.

"*I* called this meeting," the man said in a soft voice.

There is no person in New Mexico who is more greatly respected than the archbishop of the Archdiocese of Santa Fe. Certainly more honored than the state's governor or politicians, the archbishop was the highest-ranking Catholic official in the Southwest, and the presiding priest of Santa Fe's Saint Francis Cathedral.

In New Mexico, the Catholic Church had been the dominant religious body for hundreds of years. Whether willingly accepted or forced, the Church grew to be the most recognized religion of New Mexico's people. Most of the audience, whether of Catholic heritage or not, at least respected its presence.

The archbishop smiled. "I thought I needed to come. I have heard many stories in the past few days. Hurtful words and actions have opened old wounds and created new ones. I hoped I might be able to help heal the wounds before they grew worse."

Even among the Puebloans, many of whom practiced a combination of ancient native beliefs within the context of Catholicism, the archbishop was well known and respected. The Native American religions had largely adapted to the Church and its teachings long ago. The man who danced the Corn Dance on Saturday could be the same man who served at the altar on Sunday.

As he stood at the microphone, the archbishop's smile fell away and his voice grew firm. "Stop this," he said, his voice growing louder. "Stop this violence now!"

He was like a stern father with an errant child, Jennifer thought. There was no gentle persuasion or mild suggestion or pacifying the audience, just a direct, forceful message.

"No more! Violence is *never* the solution, no matter how you feel about a problem!"

He paused and then softened his voice.

"I have some news for you," he continued. "Some good news. Good news delivered in the strangest of ways. Good news that could not have even been imagined yesterday.

"We all know there have been wars between the Pueblos and the Spanish. We all know there have been wars between the Spanish and the Anglos. We all know there have been wars between the Native Americans and the Anglos. If memory serves me correctly, I believe we have all fought against one another at one time or another, and usually many times.

"That this is true, is fact. We call it history. It is hard for different people to live together, and we have *all* been different from each other at one time or another. I believe we are all still different today."

The archbishop gestured toward the audience, toward himself, and around the room.

"But I remember that we have also been the same. When we all had a common enemy. In the great wars of the world, did we not fight *for* one another? And *with* one another? Haven't we all lost fathers and brothers and daughters and friends at someone else's hands? And don't we still today have common enemies whom we fight against? The enemies of poverty, ignorance, and hunger?"

Mogi sat in the audience listening. He was remembering the fear of the past two days. He had never before felt fear like he'd felt in the thick darkness of the canyon of the hidden river.

"We cannot change four hundred years of history. We can't even change yesterday, nor today. We can only change ourselves, that tomorrow might be different from today."

There was complete silence in the lecture hall. It was a strong message, though told in a quiet voice.

"So what of our meeting tonight? What is the reason I have called you here? Have I brought justice for everyone? I'm afraid not. I do not have justice to give you. Have I brought judgment? No. I leave judgment to God. But I have brought a gift." The archbishop lifted his voice. "A gift for you. A gift, I hope, for all of us. A gift that will allow us to let our anger go, and allow our memories to take their place back in history, to rest where they belong."

Bob Toffler moved behind the archbishop with the wooden box Mogi had removed from its altar only a few hours before. The archbishop took the box and placed it before him on the podium.

"There is a story that goes with the gift. The story starts with the returning of the Spanish conquistadors in 1692, twelve years after the revolt of the Pueblos against their rule. The leaders of Acoma Pueblo were afraid of the Spanish soldiers, as were all of the Puebloan people. But the Acoma leaders had in their possession something they felt could protect them; it was an object used by the Spanish that had great power and represented the strength of the Spanish god.

"Fearing that it might be taken from them, they hid this something, this holy object, in a sacred hiding place, a place known only to a few. Unfortunately, the knowledge of that place was lost.

"You have heard from a man, a professor, who—even this week—was searching for that place and that object. He was searching for it to prove that his ideas were correct, ideas that, if true, would change how we view our ancestors."

He looked at the audience with knowing eyes and continued.

"Yesterday, the sacred place was found. And, in it, the sacred object was revealed."

There were murmurs in the crowd.

"Did this object have to do with human sacrifice?" he asked and paused. "Yes!"

The audience remained still.

"Did this object have to do with human blood?" he asked just as clearly. "Yes!" He paused again.

"Did this object have to do with eating the flesh of a human?" he asked, raising his voice at the end. "Yes!"

The audience grew loud with murmurs as the archbishop reached for the box and undid the clasps.

"Long ago, a very simple object was seen as being different from other things. An object that, even to the people who had not made it, gave witness to something beyond the ordinary. Something that was recognized as sacred."

He opened the box and removed the wrapped object.

"The Pueblo people had seen an object directly connected to the execution of a human being. At the same time, the object was worshipped as being the heart of the Spanish religion. They saw it every week, and sometimes, more often than that."

He paused again.

"But in this case," he said, relaxing his voice even more, "the object was not just connected to an execution of a human being, but to an execution of the Spanish god himself. This was the story the priests told over and over. They performed a ceremony to remember that execution. And in that ceremony, they drank the blood and ate the flesh of their god."

He unwrapped the object and placed it on top of the box. A silver chalice.

It was the chalice that was used in the Christian communion service, along with a plate that held the bread. The wine represented the blood of Christ, and the bread represented the body of Christ.

Long-stemmed, with a round base and a goblet-sized bowl, it held enough wine for several people to take a ceremonial sip.

The archbishop reached into his pocket, took out a small Bible, and turned several pages. Looking at the audience, he quoted the passage more than read it:

> *"During supper he took bread and having said the blessing he broke it and gave it to them, with the words: 'Take this; this is my body.' Then he took a cup, and having offered thanks to God he gave it to them; and they all drank from it. And he said, 'This is my blood, the blood of the covenant, shed for many.'"*

The audience was stunned.

In the 1600s, there was no word in the language of the Acoma for "chalice," or *caliz*, as the missionary priests called it in Spanish. The Indians called it by words familiar to them, words describing what they heard the priest say: The chalice was a cup holding the blood of a person executed by others.

The Acoma, with limited knowledge of Spanish and Catholic teachings, equated it with the things involved in the slaughter of animals—the bowls and jars used to catch the animal's blood as it was killed.

Blood holders.

The archbishop closed the Bible and took the silver cup in his hand. He held it up and contemplated it with his eyes.

"Do you know what I see here? I see an object that was re-garded as 'sacred' to a people who, not even knowing why, understood that some things speak of Heaven.

"Do you know what I see here? I see a number of vastly different people who all understand, in many different ways, one essential feeling that is common among us—that there are things on Earth that speak of things that are not *of* Earth, things that exist so that we lift our eyes upward, instead of inward."

The archbishop put the chalice down. He paused one more time, looking across the audience.

"We need, every day, to remember that one essential, com-mon feeling. It is what binds us to one another. It is our bond. Let us never let that bond go!

"We need to always being looking upward, instead of inward."

The archbishop then related the adventures of the four teen-agers, the original riddle, the discovery of the buried canyon and hidden river, and the shrine under the hard rock of El Malpais.

He decided to leave the skeleton until later.

Jennifer, Rachel, Mogi, and Manny were asked to stand. They received an ovation that had a flavor of not just recognition, but of relief—relief from fear and terror, relief from the pain of divided families, relief from memories.

Mogi watched as Jennifer held Manny's hand. Tears ran down his cheeks.

CHAPTER

16

The summer blew by like a gust of wind, and October came before Mogi and Jennifer were ready. The willows along the San Juan River took on a distinct gray color for fall while the Russian olive trees, never very green to start with, become even less so. The few cottonwoods turned shades of beautiful yellows and browns, eventually shedding their leaves across the countryside.

But the skies above the slickrock country were different, the smells were different, and the feelings were different, so the people of the town favored activities that encouraged things to settle down. Winter would be coming, and preparations should be made for staying indoors, huddling together for the long months of winter.

"An email from Rachel!" Jennifer called out to Mogi. He walked into the family room to hear the latest news from the land of hard-walking.

Jennifer read the email aloud from her laptop.

"You wouldn't believe the difference it's made! The Santa Fe Fiestas and Indian Market had all sorts of objects that featured images of the chalice: new pots, blankets, flags, Spanish shields, drums, coats, hats, and even license plates.

"Our chalice was used in the main celebrations of Mass for

Fiesta week, and the archbishop liked his talk at Grants so much that he whipped it into a longer version (a *much* longer version) and used it for the opening address at this year's Legislature. There wasn't a dry eye in the house.

"And you wouldn't believe who showed up, expecting to 'share the moment'—in that puke suit! He made some motions to get himself on the agenda, but my dad caught up with him. After a few subtle hints about assault, theft, and abuse of property, our professor made a hasty retreat for another state.

"Our chalice went back to the church at Acoma, where they built a special case into the side of the altar. They had to put it behind glass, though. It would make quite a prize if someone stole it.

"They still haven't identified the skeleton, but went ahead and had a burial with full honors. The governors from the pueblos even attended. They're searching the records, and I expect some story will emerge about a soldier who went out to capture a fleeing slave and never came back. The Hispanic community is acting like they've found something precious that was lost a long time ago, just like the pueblos.

"I should get back to work. I'm here for another year while I make some money for college. I got a job as the head of the Grants Chamber of Commerce. Can you believe that??????"

"I can believe that," Mogi said matter-of-factly.

"Oh, one more thing. You should be getting a package soon. Keep watch for the FedEx truck. Manny has moved back to Sky City with his grandmother and is working with an uncle to be a silversmith. He and I came up with some gifts for you two since you're now our most favorite people. We think it'll keep you guys remembering the great time you had. You wouldn't believe the change in Manny!!!!!! He's going for a GED this fall and should be done in December. And he's looking for a trade school to get into. He must have found something he didn't know he was looking for.

"Later! Thanks for everything. Keeping up with you Franklins was a riot!!!!!!!"

Jennifer laughed. What a girl. Rachel and her dad had joined them for the last days of their vacation, and they'd a ball together in Albuquerque. It wasn't hard to get Manny to come to Albuquerque for a dinner, and he even brought his mother. It was hard for everyone to say good-bye.

Two days later, FedEx delivered the package.

A large box held two small boxes, wrapped carefully in cornhusks and tied with long, narrow strips of blanket yarn. Waiting for each other to open their boxes, Mogi and Jennifer carefully unwrapped layers of soft deerskin to reveal identical silver chalices, about four inches high, duplicates of the original blood holder.

Mogi went to his room and placed his chalice on his desk, giving it a shine with the tail of his shirt. Jennifer came in to watch.

"You know," Mogi said thoughtfully, "I may have to go help him paint his car."

Jennifer just laughed.

NOW AVAILABLE
Book 5 of the Mogi Franklin Mysteries: The Lake of Fire

On a school nature trip near the national laboratory at Los Alamos, Mogi Franklin learns of the mysterious disappearance fifty years before of a plane carrying 200 pounds of plutonium. In *The Lake of Fire,* the fifth book of the Mogi Franklin Mysteries, he soon is involved in a complex web of government lies, terrorist nations, and a hunt for the missing material—until a sudden firestorm puts the town and mountains around it in the path of a raging inferno.

ABOUT THE AUTHOR

Don Willerton was raised in a small oil boomtown in the Panhandle of Texas, becoming familiar through family vacations with the northern New Mexico area where he now makes his home.

After earning a degree in physics from Midwestern State University in Texas and a master's in computer science and electrical engineering from the University of New Mexico, he worked for Los Alamos National Laboratory for almost three decades.

During his career there, Willerton was a supercomputer programmer for a number of years and a manager after that for "way too long," and also worked on information policy and cyber-security.

He finds focusing on only one thing very difficult among such varied interests as home building, climbing Colorado's tallest peaks, and rafting the rivers of the Southwest (including the Colorado through Grand Canyon). Willerton also has owned a handyman business for a number of years, rebuilt old cars, and made furniture in his woodshop.

About the Author

He is a wanderer in both mind and body, fascinated with history and its landscape, varied peoples and their cultures, good mysteries, secrets, and seeking out treasure. Most of all, he loves the outdoors and the places he finds in the Southwest where spirits live and ghosts dance. Weaving it all together to share with readers has been the driving force of Willerton's writing over the past twenty years.

The Hidden River is the fourth novel in the nine-book Mogi Franklin series of Southwest-based mysteries for middle-grade boys and girls.